MW01591502

Dark Summer

THE WITCHLING TRILOGY, BOOK ONE

Lizzy Ford

Copyright ©2012 Lizzy Ford
http://www.GuerrillaWordfare.com/

Edited by Christine LePorte
http://www.ChristineLePorte.com/

Cover art and design by Indie Designz
http://www.indiedesignz.com/

Dark Summer copyright © 2012 by Lizzy Ford
Cover art and design copyright 2012 by Indie Designz

Published by Kettlecorn Press/Guerrilla Wordfare
ISBN: 978-1-62378-027-2

Dedication

As always, a heartfelt thank you goes out to:

My husband, Matt, whose support is vital to my success

My graphics designer (and sweet friend!), Dafeenah

My editor and mentor, Christine

Jenn, who keeps me on my toes and out of trouble

Also by Lizzy Ford

The Rhyn Trilogy
Katie's Hellion, Book I (May 2011)
Katie's Hope, Book II (September 2011)
Rhyn's Redemption, Book III (March 2012)

Rhyn Eternal Series
Gabriel's Hope (September 2012)

The War of Gods series
Damian's Oracle (October 2011)
Damian's Assassin (November 2011)
Damian's Immortal (December 2011)
The Grey God (May 2012)

The Foretold Trilogy
Elle's Journey (December 2011)
Shadow Rising (Winter 2012)

Anshan Saga
Kiera's Moon (June 2011)
Kiera's Sun (Fall 2012)

Single-titles
A Demon's Desire
The Warlord's Secret
Maddy's Oasis
Rebel Heart

The Witchling Trilogy
Dark Summer (late summer 2012)
Autumn Storm (autumn 2012)
Winter Kiss (winter 2013)

Chapter One

SUMMER STEPPED OFF the stuffy bus, at once struck by the smog-free air and towering pine trees of the northern Idaho town. The sun shone gentler here than in her native Los Angeles, and the heat of noon was pleasant.

The bus driver pulled her bags from the storage compartment under the bus and left them beside her. She didn't meet his eyes, not wanting to tell him she had no tip money. The orphanage had paid for her trip via Greyhound and given her a meager ten dollars a day for food.

"My sister lives up here. She tells everyone to avoid the forest after dark," the bus driver said cheerfully.

Summer sneaked a look at him. He didn't look upset at her for not tipping, and he said nothing else about his odd warning. He boarded the bus with a smile, and the lumbering vehicle merged back onto the single, two lane road hedged by pine trees running through Priest Lake, Idaho. She looked at the run down school in whose parking lot she stood. It was closed down for the summer, the cement of the parking lot cracked and the field behind overgrown with grass.

A warm breeze swept by her. It smelled of trees and burning wood. Something else was in the air, something that tickled her body from the inside out. The breeze seemed to return and swirl around her, lifting the hem of her shirt and jeans. She pushed her top down self-consciously.

"Ignore that."

She looked up into the most beautiful eyes she'd ever seen. The teen walking towards her from the street was around seventeen with breeze-ruffled brown hair and eyes as clear and teal as footage of the Caribbean she'd seen on TV. His smile was bright and friendly, his skin and facial features indicating he was of Native American heritage. Around six feet tall, he'd begun to fill out, and his arms were muscular in the snug T-shirt he wore.

"You'll understand in a few days. This isn't a normal town."

She couldn't find her voice. Aware of how hard she was staring at him, she looked away as heat spread across her face.

"I'm Beck, the good half of the Turner twins. You'll hear about us, I'm sure. You have a name?" he asked.

She nodded.

"Well, what is it?" he asked with another of his infectious smiles.

"Summer," she whispered.

"Welcome, Summer." He extended his hand.

She hesitated then shook her head, withdrawing.

2

"No worries," he said. "But, just so you know, whatever your gift is, it's okay here. We all have them."

Summer looked up at him again, surprised.

"Come on. I was supposed to get my driver's license last spring, but, well, stuff happens. If I had known I'd be stuck walking to and from here picking up new people *all* summer long, I would've gotten it," he said with a sigh. He reached forward to take her suitcase and began walking towards the road.

She followed, curious about his statement about a town of gifted people.

"We all live at the boarding school," Beck continued. He grunted as he lifted her suitcase from the parking lot onto the road. "Do you play any sports?"

"No."

"Cheerleader?"

"No."

"Band?"

"No."

"What do you do?"

"Nothing really." *Except get ridiculed and kicked out of school after school for being different.* She hadn't had time to learn a sport, not when she switched schools every other month. The orphanage had run out of schools to send her to in Los Angeles and Orange County and banished her here. Beck wouldn't call her magick a *gift* when he saw what it did and how little she could control it. It acted out everywhere she went, sometimes knocking over full rooms of people as if they were shoved by an invisible hand and sometimes doing much more damage, like the fire two schools ago.

Summer looked straight up at the sky, marveling at the tall trees lining the road. The road itself looked worn and run down like the school, with faded lane lines and potholes filled with grass. The forest seemed to be trying to reclaim the human invasion. It had swallowed what might've one time been a sidewalk alongside the road and replaced it with orange, waist high tiger lilies and white daisies. Birds were loud without the constant drone of LA traffic.

She liked the feel of nature. Its subtle magick hummed in the air around her. Her eyes went to the forest again. She caught the movement of grasses and branches as someone with bright auburn hair darted from the gutter into the forest. Summer squinted, trying to see into the woods. She sensed someone there but saw no one.

Beck's soft laughter drew her attention. He was a good twenty feet ahead of her. She'd stopped in place and gotten lost in her head.

"Come on!" he said and began walking again.

Summer hurried to catch up, embarrassed at what the handsome boy might think of her after just five minutes with her. She always made the worst impressions. Staring at the ground, she focused on ignoring the woody magick and just walking. Like a normal person. Like someone who wasn't cursed with magick in her blood.

They walked farther than she expected, past a small string of ranch style houses, driveways to hidden homes, and a tiny strip mall with a convenience market, gas station and realtor's office. They kept walking until the road forked and the forest closed in on either side once again.

At last, they reached a dirt road leading off the paved street into the forest. Beck said a few curse words that made her blush as he struggled to roll her suitcase on the dirt road. Summer watched, amused, before her eyes went to the trees.

4

They were so tall, their tops almost met in the middle of the sky above her.

Beck's loudest curse yet drew her eyes to him again. He shoved the suitcase onto its side, his earlier good humor turned into frustration.

"I'll bring one of the guys back to help me," he said. "I'll take you there first."

Summer drew near her suitcase, not wanting to leave the few things she did have. Mementos from her mother and father were in there, along with the pictures of the very few friends she'd made over the past sixteen years. Clothing, trinkets, an amulet from the only teacher who didn't turn on her ...

"I'll help you," she said and bent to grab the bar at the bottom of the suitcase.

"This isn't LA. No one will take your stuff," he said.

"I don't want to leave it."

"Are you sure?" He looked her over. "You're kinda small."

She flushed as his eyes lingered on her breasts. She was small—in every way but *that* one.

"I can do it," she said.

"Well, it's my fault anyway for not getting a driver's license," he said with a frown. "Fine. I'll use my ESP to call my brother."

She waited to see him reach for a cell phone. He closed his eyes, held out his arms and went perfectly still for a few seconds.

"Just kidding. I don't have ESP," he said with another grin. "He was supposed to meet me at the school. He should be here soon. Don't be surprised. Decker's a little – "

"A little what, Beck?"

Summer turned to see the second Turner twin stepping out of the forest. Decker looked identical to Beck, except his eyes were as black as his clothing. Forest shadows seemed to cling to him, and she stepped back as he approached. Decker didn't smile like Beck did.

"I knew you'd be prowling the forests. A little help," Beck said, indicating the suitcase.

"This wouldn't keep happening if you'd gotten your driver's license."

"You don't have yours either."

The twins glared at each other before Decker strode forward. He and Beck reached for the suitcase and lifted it.

"Her name is Summer, by the way," Beck said.

"Has she – " Decker started to ask.

"No, Decker. Obviously, she just got here. She's from an orphanage in LA, and I think this is the first time she's ever been anywhere with trees. She's sixteen."

"Let the girl tell her own story, Beck," Decker snapped.

Uncertain what to do with the tension between them, Summer said nothing.

"*Do* you talk?" Decker asked, turning his attention to her for the first time. Though he was as handsome as his brother, his abrasive manner reminded her too much of the bullies she'd dealt with her whole life.

"Leave her alone," Beck replied.

Thank you! she cried silently to the nicer of the twins. Beck was hot and sweet. She'd never met someone quite like him.

They walked in silence down the winding road. The rocks made her twist her ankle more than once. She'd worn sandals, not expecting to hike to get where they were going, and blisters were forming on her heels. She tried not to limp, not wanting to cause even more trouble to them.

A sprawling log building came into view finally and she sighed. It grew larger the closer they got, until they stood on the front porch. Feet aching, Summer sat on the stairs of the porch and pulled off the sandals. The back of her heels were bloodied. She grimaced at the stinging pain.

"Why didn't you tell her to change shoes before dragging her three miles?" Decker demanded of his brother as they placed her suitcase down.

"I don't know what she's wearing."

The two stood over her. Summer shifted away and stood.

"I'm okay," she said, holding her sandals in her hand.

"I'll show you where the bathroom is," Decker said and swung open the screen door.

"I'm sorry, Summer," Beck said as she passed. "I'll get you checked in. The girls stay in the main house, so you don't have to walk anymore."

She smiled up at him, caught by his teal gaze. He held the screen door open for her, and she paused in the doorway, letting her eyes adjust. The door opened into a tall foyer flanked by an open living area on one side and a formal dining room with a table that stretched thirty feet on the other side. The house was log on the inside, too, making it feel warm and welcoming.

It was nothing like the orphanage, with its cement floors and walls and yard sale furniture. She took in the comfortable, worn leather furniture in the living area featuring a stone hearth and a huge flat screen television mounted on a wall. There were chairs everywhere, as if a group of people had been gathered around to watch a show.

7

Decker was standing in front of a door down a hall ahead of her, waiting impatiently. She moved into the house. The floors were wooden, covered in thick rugs that quieted her steps.

"Thank you," she murmured to the darker twin. The bathroom was huge with a small sofa on one wall, several stalls and a row of polished bronzed sinks on top of dark cabinets.

"Sit down," Decker said with abruptness. He followed her in and opened one cabinet after the other until he found what he sought.

Summer sat down on the couch. He filled a plastic bowl with warm water and a wash cloth and brought it to her.

"Oh, seriously?" Beck demanded, standing in the doorway. "Starting a little early, aren't you?"

"You want me to let her bleed to death?" Decker shot back.

"This won't change anything."

"Then why are you complaining?"

The Turner twins glared at each other, bristling. Summer stared at them, not understanding what the issue was. They looked ready to fight.

"I can do it," she said and took the bowl. "Thank you both."

"You heard her," Beck said and stepped aside, motioning to the door.

"After you, brother."

They left. Summer waited for the door to close then shook her head. Whatever sibling rivalry was between the two, they had it bad. She dipped a foot in the warm water and tried to work the blood off without touching her raw heel with the washcloth.

"I told the Turners to get their licenses," a woman said with a sigh.

Summer looked up as a pretty woman in a flowing dress entered. She was barefoot, and her ankle bracelets jingled with each step. She wore a dazzling turquoise necklace that matched her eyes.

"I'm Amber, one of those who will be overseeing your education. You must be Summer."

Summer nodded.

"I hope the Turner twins didn't scare you off already." Amber laughed.

Summer shook her head. She liked Amber. The blond woman had a large smile and sparkling eyes. Amber brought her a towel and sat cross-legged on the floor a few feet away.

"Our school is for children with special gifts that keep them from integrating into normal schools. A lot of behavioral issues are simply a lack of understanding by mainstream teachers about how unique some of you are."

"What do you mean?" Summer asked. "I don't have behavioral issues."

"We'll talk about it more later," Amber promised. "For now, just know this is a safe environment. We operate classes year round. The summer schedule is very relaxed, more like a college environment than the typical high school schedule. I think you'll enjoy it."

Summer looked down at her feet. She dried them without speaking. She'd never lasted more than two months in any one school. It was not a matter of her enjoying it; it was a matter of her and everyone around her surviving it.

So far, she really, really liked this place. It was beautiful and peaceful. Beck was the best-looking guy she'd ever seen, and Amber was far friendlier than any teacher Summer had ever had. With a heavy heart, she realized she couldn't get attached. In a month or two, people would realize what she was. They'd turn against her, as usual, and this wonderful place with the magickal breeze would be gone from her life.

"I'll show you to your room," Amber said.

Summer trailed her through the house and up a set of stairs that led to a second floor lined with doors. She heard the sounds of giggling from behind some of the doors and at least one television as she passed. Amber led her to the end of the hall and opened a door. Summer expected to see the sparse, prison-like sagging metal bunks of the orphanage and was surprised to see two twin beds separated by a nightstand. There was carpet in the bedroom, dressers on either wall, and closets. One dresser was littered with makeup and perfume. The windows above the beds were open, the blue-edged, white curtains matching the fluffy comforters on the bed.

She'd never seen a bed that looked so comfortable!

"Your roommate's name is Trinity," Amber said. "She's on vacation with her family right now. She'll be back before school starts in about a month."

Summer's suitcase was already beside her dresser. She set her purse on the bed and pressed her hand into the comforter.

"Dinner is at six downstairs. We have a few basic rules," Amber continued. "Dinner is mandatory during weekdays. After dark fall, no one leaves the house without an adult escort. Breakfast hours are from seven to nine and lunch from eleven to one. We keep chefs on staff, so you can order whatever you want. No smoking, no drugs, no candles, no pets, no food in the rooms. The television downstairs goes off every night at ten, but you can stay up as late as you want in your room. There's also a shuttle that leaves hourly to the store, resort, and a few other small stops around town."

DARK SUMMER

Summer listened. She walked to the window beside her bed and pushed aside the curtains, gazing into the backyard hedged by two long rows of dorms. In the center were several fire pits, barbecues and picnic tables. As she watched, she saw the Turner twins appear. Beck went to the table with kids wearing jeans and shorts while Decker went to the table where everyone wore black. Two barbecues were going, and the kids at both tables were eating and laughing.

Where the property ended, the forest was thick and the trees swaying. She saw it again, the movement of someone darting into the forest.

"You can go down, if you'd like."

Summer jumped at the nearness of Amber's voice.

"No, thank you," she said.

"Go down and meet people," Amber insisted. "The Turner twins will introduce you around."

Summer's gaze went to the forest again. Someone was following her, had been since the bus left her. She nodded.

Satisfied, Amber smiled, saying, "Change shoes and go. Don't be shy!"

She left. Summer opened her suitcase and pulled out another pair of sandals, these sliding between her toes so as not to hurt her heels. She left the room and trotted down the stairs, exiting the front door.

Her new world amazed her. She found herself waiting to feel the magick she'd sensed at the school and gazing at the trees. The dirt road continued past the long dorms towards the forest. She walked to the end of the dorms then looked into the forest where she'd seen the dark figure disappear.

Summer stepped into the forest, at once intrigued by the sense of magick in the swaying trees. Sunlight splashed through the pine canopy onto bright purple bluebells that

11

layered the forest floor. Small bushes hunched against trees and one another, and Summer stopped to try a few tart berries.

Continuing into the forest, she watched startled birds flit away above her. The brilliant color of a blue jay made her forget whoever it was following her. She followed the bird through the forest and into a small meadow filled with wildflowers.

She'd ever been anywhere as beautiful or magickal. Grinning, she ran across the meadow then twirled around in the middle of it, spinning amidst the wildflowers as she stared up at the blue sky. The breeze joined her, throwing her hair around her while filling her again with the warm, tickling sensation.

A dark figure crossed her vision. She stumbled and fell, seeking out the shape she'd seen. No one was there. She pushed herself up. A deep growl made her turn. Staring at her through golden eyes, a sand colored cougar crouched on the other side of the meadow. Its tail twitched.

Summer froze. The animal raised itself and took a step closer. Her heart hammered in her breast. She looked beyond it to the trees then recalled how foolish it would be to try to climb a tree to escape. A beast like this lived in trees.

The growl came again. The great cat lowered itself, bunching its body in a sign it was preparing to pounce.

Summer whirled and ran. The auburn-haired figure ahead of her disappeared into the forest. The growling and sound of pursuit stopped suddenly. She glanced over her shoulder and slowed. The cougar was gone. She pressed her shaking hands to her face.

It was early for hallucinations. She'd only just arrived.

"What're you doing here?"

12

She looked up, dismayed to see Decker there. He lingered at the edge of the forest, as if sunlight would disable the shadows guarding him. His piercing gaze was on her.

"I was just exploring," she managed at last.

"Do you know the way back?"

The way he said it made her want to tell him she did, so he'd leave her alone. Summer gazed around her. The forest looked the same in each direction of the meadow. She'd been too absorbed in the forest magick to consider where she went.

"I'm guessing no," Decker said. "I've had to rescue you twice today."

"I'm fine," she replied. "It can't be that hard."

"Until a cougar corners you."

She stared at him.

"They're usually nocturnal. The wildfires are driving them out during daylight. You should probably come back with me."

She shivered, sensing danger from him, the same danger she'd felt from the cougar. Only instead of pouncing on her, Decker wanted to lure her somewhere. The idea made no sense. Just because he dressed all in black didn't mean he was any more of a threat than his more cheerful brother.

"C'mon." He turned and walked into the forest.

With another look around, Summer trailed.

"You're rooming with Trinity?" he asked.

"Yes."

"When's your birthday?"

"Next month."

"So is mine." He stopped to look at her curiously. "What date?"

"Twentieth."

"I'm on the nineteenth. I'll be eighteen. I assume you'll be seventeen. Turning seventeen is a big deal here," he told her and continued walking.

"Seventeen? I thought most people considered sixteen the big year."

"Not here."

They reached the edge of the forest and the school property. He headed for the picnic tables, but she stopped.

"There's food," he said over his shoulder.

"No thanks."

"You're on your own. Stay out of the forest."

Irritated at his rebuke, she trudged to the road that wrapped around the dorms, not wanting to meet anyone just yet. Chances were, she'd be gone soon anyway. No use making friends. She went back to her room, and her spirits brightened. She'd never had her own room, even if this one was hers alone for a month.

Summer flung herself across the bed, sinking into it with a deep sigh. She'd never had such comfortable bedding, such a peaceful place to sleep. She eyed the dresser. While she'd had dressers, she'd never unpacked.

She unzipped her suitcase and pulled out the old wooden jewelry box holding her treasures. Her eyes went to the pile of jewelry and makeup on Trinity's dresser. Summer tentatively set her box on her own dresser and sat down, staring at it. It looked lonely and small.

Her sense of anxiety grew again, and she took it down. She didn't know how long she'd stay; it was easier to keep everything packed up. Picking out her least worn clothing, she set it on the bed for dinner then set her alarm and lay down for a nap.

Chapter Two

"HEY, DECKER."

On the porch lining one side of the dorms, Decker turned at his twin's voice. Beck was in the doorway of their shared dorm room. Dawn, Beck's blond girlfriend, winked as she slinked from the room back towards the teens in the Square, the barbecue and hangout area between the two dorms. Beck watched her then disappeared into their room.

Decker altered his course and entered the room. Beck closed the door behind him.

"What're you doing?" Beck demanded.

"Talking to you."

"Cut the crap. You're making moves on the new girl. You know you can't influence her decisions."

"You're welcome." Decker replied and folded his arms. "Your little friend would've been eaten by a cougar if I hadn't found her in the forest. But you wouldn't know that, because your head is in Dawn's tits."

Beck looked surprised then grew red. "I'm in love with her. I can't really help it."

"She's using you the same way she used me. Dawn doesn't *love* us. She *loves* our family's money."

"No, Decker. Your soul is too black to understand."

It was Decker's turn to grow angry. He flung himself on his bed to keep from punching his brother, who'd gotten on his nerves too much lately.

"You should leave Summer alone," Beck said with more firmness. "She's a good girl. She doesn't need you corrupting her."

"I don't corrupt anyone, anymore than you do. Sam told me to look after her, and I will."

"Sam did? When? Why?"

"You know he only tells us what he wants us to know," Decker snapped.

"You didn't ask him what you were protecting her from?"

"Why? I can handle anything that comes here."

"No, Decker, you can't! You're not eighteen yet. We're no different than any other witchlings until we turn eighteen."

Decker knew as much but said nothing. There really wasn't anything the two of them couldn't handle, if he could get Beck to take his responsibilities seriously instead of acting like the lovesick fool. Still, they didn't have the magick they would when they inherited their titles. Beck would become the Master of Light and Decker, the Master of Fire and Night. Each was responsible for claiming the souls of witchlings to balance the scale between good and evil in the world.

Highly competitive, they'd both begun to dig their claws into newcomers a year before. It escalated into a fist fight one night three months ago, which earned them both disciplinary action at the school and suspension of privileges from their parents. Both were forbidden from getting their driver's licenses, and Decker had his motorcycle taken away. They'd both been forced to stay at the school for the summer, instead of joining their jet setting parents on their summer vacations to Europe.

"She belongs to the Light," Beck said.

"I can't disobey Sam."

"I'm telling you, Decker, back off. Whatever is after her, it can't get her on school grounds. They're protected."

"Right, because she knows that. You know how it is the first few weeks here, Beck. No one tells you what's going on. It's part of Amber's *self-discovery* crap."

"It's worked for twenty years. Leave her alone, Decker." Beck stormed out and slammed the door behind him.

Decker winced. His elements were water, fire and spirit. Whenever there were people in the Square between the dorms, he got headaches from the clamor of their spirits. He waited until he'd cooled down enough not to punch Beck if his twin was outside.

Decker opened the door and left, slipping into the forest. He was most at home in the forest after dark, when he could hide in the shadows of night, and the sounds and people awake during the day were gone. His headache eased as he walked deeper into the forest. He wasn't about to tell Beck the other reason he'd followed the new girl. Nothing scared him since his motorcycle accident a year and a half ago, when he'd plowed into a rock wall in the middle of the night and lay dying for hours before someone found him.

But he'd met her twice now and knew without a doubt: Summer wasn't just special, she was somehow connected to him. Her aura shimmered with innocence and fear, a strange combination until he found out she was an orphan. Her soul was sad, but she'd been nice. Large brown eyes, delicate features, a shapely body just blooming into womanhood ... she'd caught his attention with her looks only after he felt the power trapped within her. He shouldn't feel drawn to Summer, but he did. The effects of physical attraction he knew already. But this was something different, deeper.

Lost in thought, he didn't hear the approach of the forest creature, Sam, until it spoke.

The future Master of Fire and Dark comes to visit.

"Not here for you, Sam," Decker said, not wanting to deal with anyone at the moment, even the auburn yeti standing behind him.

But I was waiting for you, the creature said into his head.

Decker turned and looked up at the creature that was a full foot taller than his six-foot-two frame. The half-man, half-ape creature offered a smile that would terrify most people.

"You didn't tell me there's something ... weird about her," he said, agitated.

No stranger than any other newcomer.

"Right. Which is why you asked me to protect her. You should've asked Beck. He's pissed at both of us now."

The creature shrugged, unconcerned.

"Why is she special, Sam?" Decker demanded.

You know why.

"No, I don't."

She may be the one who can reset the balance between good and evil.

"Reset it? How? Why?"

18

When you are the official Master of Fire and Night, I will tell you.

"I'm so sick of this place."

Did you feel a connection to her?

Decker hesitated to respond but nodded after a moment.

Trust yourself, Decker.

"I can't. My dreams are so dark and my waking life is filled with this clamor. I never have a moment of peace!" he said. "Why else do you think I ran into a cliff? It wasn't on purpose, like everyone thinks. The demons in my head drove me to it."

I know. I found you.

"You did. You're the only one who didn't turn on me after the issue at the hospital." Decker calmed some at the reminder that he wasn't entirely alone.

Then trust me when I say to trust yourself. The yeti let out a chortle of amusement. *Every Dark Master or Mistress needs a counterbalance, or the world will plummet into chaos. Your mother has your father. Evil cannot be stopped, only contained, balanced.*

"I don't feel evil, Sam."

You are not. No one is evil. But evil is within us all.

"I know, I know. Choices, yadda, yadda." Decker rolled his eyes. "I've heard this a million times before."

Because you don't listen well. Sam laughed again.

Decker let a smile slip free. The ugly creature always found a way to put him at ease and make his looming fate feel a little less terrifying. In two weeks, when he took on his new role, he'd spend the next twenty-plus years hunting down rogue witchlings who broke the Dark Laws and Light Laws and claiming their souls, like his mother did now.

"You said you were waiting for me. What's up?" he asked.

It's about your brother.

Decker's mood soured immediately.

You must protect him, too.

"Beck doesn't need me to help him."

But he does. He is not like you. He doesn't understand the Dark as you do.

"I don't understand it well."

He doesn't understand it at all.

"I'll keep an eye on him."

Good. You'll know when something is amiss.

"He doesn't listen to me," Decker warned.

The threat is not one he can fight.

"I hate my life. I couldn't just be a normal seventeen year old on his way to college this fall."

Sam grumbled a chuckle.

"I'm outta here, Sam."

The yeti raised his hand in farewell. Decker turned away and lost himself in the woods, not wanting to deal with anyone. His mind kept going to Summer and the strange draw. He didn't know what was going on, but things were likely going to get weird.

Summer's alarm went off at a quarter 'til six, just in time for dinner. She changed clothes and washed her face before descending the stairs to the main floor. The dinner table was a chorus of talk, and she crossed her arms as she entered, expecting her appearance to silence everyone. No one seemed to notice her, and her eyes went around the table as she looked for empty seats. Those sitting around the table ranged between twelve and close to twenty, young men and women that seemed divided between those in black and those in bright colors.

Beck caught her eye and waved her over. The seat between him and his brother was empty. Summer claimed it, drawing the attention of those around them. She received a few curious looks before they returned to talking. Beck was engaged in conversation with the person on his other side while Decker sat silent, brooding. For the first time since meeting him, she almost felt sorry for him. He seemed out of place among the others, a shadow.

"Thank you for helping me in the forest," she said.

Decker glanced at her. "Whatever."

Summer stared at her plate. A moment later, someone placed soup and a salad before her. She ate fast after the long bus trip. A bread basket was passed around, and she devoured two slices of the warm, homemade bread.

When the waiter placed a heaping plate of food before her, she thought she'd gone to heaven. The orphanage fed them enough to keep them alive and to keep state doctors from cutting the state funding. Summer leaned low over her plate and wolfed down the roast beef, mashed potatoes and green beans before reaching for two more pieces of bread.

"They didn't feed you often, did they?" the girl across from her said.

Summer dropped the bread and sat back, embarrassed to see the looks of those around her. Most of them had barely started on their main courses while her plate was empty.

"Take it," the girl said and pushed the bread basket towards her. "I'm Dawn."

"Summer."

"You want my beans? I hate them."

21

Summer shook her head. Her stomach was still growling, but she forced herself to put her hands in her lap. The waiter reappeared with a smile to take her plate and replace it with a huge piece of warm pie à la mode.

"Huckleberries," Beck said to her. "We pick them in the forest, and the chef makes pies."

Summer took her first bite and almost sighed. Tarter than a blueberry, the warm huckleberry filling was sweetened just enough to take the edge off while the ice cream finished balancing it out. She ate slowly, savoring the flavors and textures. When it was gone, she felt satisfied for the first time in a long time. She leaned back in her chair.

"You do eat a lot for someone so little," Beck teased, flashing the smile that made her knees weak.

"I think I know where it all goes," Dawn said, staring at Summer's chest. "You're almost popping out there. We go shopping on the weekends. You can come get some more clothes with us."

Summer's face grew hot. She crossed her arms. She'd worn a V-cut shirt, the nicest she owned, for her first dinner. If she'd had the money for clothes, she might not be wearing the same things she'd been wearing since she was fourteen. Dawn was right; nothing fit her, even her nicest clothes.

She rose and left the table, going outside to the front porch. The evening was cool, the shadows of the forest stretching across the road. Though it was August, the skies were already growing dark at seven. She sat on the stairs. The sounds of talk and laughter drifted to her from the house, and she gazed into the forest. The evening was quiet.

"Dawn's a bitch."

Summer twisted to see Decker closing the door.

"She's jealous. She's had her eye on Beck for, like, ever. If he smiles at another girl, she goes psycho."

"She's right. My clothes don't fit right," Summer replied and crossed her arms again.

"None of the guys are going to complain."

She smiled. Both the sense of danger and commonality returned. Decker sat on the other side of the stairs from her.

"The orphanage must've been rough." For the first time since meeting, he was looking at her intently.

"It was."

"Don't you have any family?"

"None that wants me."

"I'd like to say you're lucky to be here, but ..." He drifted off. "None of us are lucky to be here."

"It's beautiful and peaceful."

"I guess."

"Are you and Beck orphans?"

"No. Our father bought this place. He owns half of Manhattan. Dumped us off here for the summer."

"This is the nicest place I've ever been," she said honestly.

"It's alright. I guess we're lucky to have a family." He pulled something out of his bag. "Anyway, I brought you these. You don't have to wear them. I hate the way Dawn picks on people." He held out three neatly folded T-shirts.

She took them.

"See ya." He rose and returned to the house.

Summer looked at the T-shirts. While plain, they were soft and worn, the material fine and smooth. They weren't cheap like the donations she got at the orphanage. Touched by the kindness of the aloof boy, she hadn't wanted to upset him by saying no. She looked down at her exposed bosom then at the shirts. They smelled like fabric softener and him.

She returned to her room and put them in her suitcase with the rest of her treasures. A knock on her door came a moment before Dawn entered.

"I just wanted to apologize," Dawn said. "I meant to tease you, not drive you off. Like, every girl here would love to have you know ... your chest."

Summer said nothing, uncertain of the girl's sincerity after Decker's comments. Dawn was beautiful in the way Summer envisioned a cheerleader: athletic, golden skin, blond hair, green eyes, and a size zero. She reminded Summer of the daughters of rich parents she'd seen at one of the private schools the orphanage sent her to. There was no reason she could see for the pretty girl to be jealous.

"We're going to roast marshmallows and make s'mores," Dawn continued. "Grab a sweater and come out back!" She left.

Summer opened her suitcase. She didn't need sweaters in LA. She had one long-sleeved shirt, though after Dawn's comments at dinner, she feared wearing it. It had been too big for her when she was fourteen but now stretched too tightly over her breasts. Her gaze lingered on the T-shirts Decker had given her. She changed into one, relieved that it was big enough not to stretch over her chest.

Several of the teens from the house had already gathered around a raging bonfire. Petrified wood stumps and flat boulders acted as natural seating around the rugged fire pit, and all the seats were taken. A few of the kids had marshmallows on sticks already while a s'mores station at the picnic table consisted of stacks of chocolate and graham crackers. Summer watched one of them make a sandwich by piling a marshmallow on top of a graham cracker then layering chocolate and another cracker.

"Here," Beck said, realizing she was there. He rose and handed her the long metal marshmallow holder. "You ever have s'mores in the city?"

"No," she said. She sat down next to Dawn, whose smile went from adoring at Beck to forced when directed at Summer.

"They're the best food in the world," Dawn said. "I like mine burnt."

Her marshmallow caught on fire, and she blew it out. Summer watched her own marshmallow near the fire. Beck sat beside her.

"How do you like it here so far?" he asked.

"It's nice," she replied.

"Is the orphanage like this?"

"Not even close."

"Are you here for the summer or for the school year, too?"

"I don't know," Summer admitted. "As long as Amber wants me to stay, I guess."

"I hope it's awhile," he said with one of the smiles that made her melt.

Summer flushed. "I hope so, too."

"Marshmallow's on fire."

She yanked it free and blew on it, as Dawn had, before standing and going to the table. Dawn smiled as she passed and sat beside Beck. Summer began to think Decker was just too moody; Dawn had been nothing but nice since the incident at dinner.

Carefully, Summer set her crispy marshmallow on a cracker, stacked chocolate and another cracker and lifted it. Her first bite made her frown. It didn't taste like any of the ingredients. It tasted like ... fish? She took another bite. Same thing.

"You like it?" Beck called.

"Not really," she replied. "It doesn't taste right."

"Let me see." He held out his hand.

She gave it to him. He took a bite.

"Tastes fine to me," he said. "Maybe it's just not something you like?"

"I guess," she said, disappointed.

Dawn offered a smile. Summer tossed the rest of her s'more and sat near the fire on the ground. The dancing flames and her full stomach from dinner made her drowsy. The kids around her talked while she sat in silence. Decker wasn't there this evening. None of the kids in black were, and she wondered if they had their own campfire.

Dawn and Beck were hanging all over one another, and they rose together, walking hand-in-hand into the forest.

So much for that, Summer thought to herself. The two were a perfect match. With brown eyes and hair and her short stature, she'd never compete with a cheerleader like Dawn. Beck was a gentleman, though, and she could appreciate how he'd made her feel in the time they spent together.

Summer left quietly and walked to the front of the house, chilled by the evening coolness. She sat on the porch again, looking up. The moon was a sliver overhead, and there were more stars in the small patch of sky above than she'd ever seen in the LA skies. A movement down the driveway caught her attention.

Someone was there. He looked huge, standing in the middle of the driveway. There was no mistaking this for a shadow or a trick of her eyes. From the distance, he looked ... furry, a cross between a man and an ape with auburn hair that covered his body. She stared at him. He stared back. After along moment, he darted again into the forest.

It had to be the hallucinations. The possibility that there was a bigfoot living in the forest, stalking her, didn't seem as plausible as a wild invention of her tired mind.

Summer fled inside and closed the door to her room. She huddled in her bed under the covers, waiting for the monster to get her.

Chapter Three

THE NEXT MORNING, she sat outside with Amber, whose words sounded like the plot some sort of movie. Amber had repeated them three times so far, and each time, Summer felt as if they grew more and more foreign.

"Could you say that again?" she asked.

Amber smiled. "Everyone here possesses some sort of magick. Some will cross to Dark magick and some will stay in the Light. The balance between good and evil in the world is struck right here, in Priest Lake."

Summer stared at her blankly.

"We train all witchlings together in how to use their magick. We test them, and wherever their decisions lead them is which side they ultimately serve."

The words still seemed ... crazy.

"I teach those who stay in the Light and those who are newly arrived, before they choose. Speaking of which, are you ready for your first class?" Amber asked. She pushed open a door in on the bottom floor of the house. "Dance."

The clash of reality and this strange new world left Summer speechless. She followed Amber into the dance studio, her own reflection catching along one wall. The girls in the room wore dance attire, either snug clothing or leotards. Summer's attention went from Amber's strange words to her own baggy sweatpants with holes and an oversized T-shirt. She crossed her arms again as the eyes of the dozen girls in the class fell to her. A few of them smiled, while the others went back to stretching.

Amber took up a spot near the back of class. A woman who looked as young as any of them stepped forward to lead them in some basic stretches and ballet moves. Summer's body responded despite the stretch of time between now and the ballet classes she took as a child, before entering the state system. She focused on moving instead of thinking, unable to digest exactly what it was Amber was trying to tell her.

She remembered the basics, stumbled a few times, but grew proud of herself for mastering the simple moves better than even Dawn. Amber smiled her encouragement.

"Dance is about understanding your body," the instructor, Jessie, said. "It's about identifying, controlling and mastering every muscle. For those practicing magick, it's the starting point for becoming in tune with your body, so you can recognize where your magick resides."

More about magick. Summer tried to ignore the *magick* and focus on the movements. She'd learned to listen to her body during the long nights she spent at the orphanage, when she could neither sleep nor concentrate on reading or anything else.

The instructor finished the stretches and turned on music. Summer was surprised to hear the heavy beats and high-pitched strumming of Middle Eastern music. She watched as the instructor began to teach simple neck, hip and knee circles before moving into hip flips and other movements, ending with undulations.

Embarrassed, Summer stood awkwardly while the others around her tried the moves, some laughing when they fell or fumbled while others concentrated hard. The instructor caught her eye. Summer looked away fast but not fast enough; the instructor approached her while the others struggled with the moves.

"Newbie?" she asked Amber.

"Very. And shy," Amber said with another smile of encouragement towards Summer.

"Teen girls are never comfortable with their bodies," Jessie said. "You'll find that Amber and I have similar styles of teaching. Let your body do what it feels it should. If you can move the thinking out of the way, you'll feel the music, the same way you feel the magick."

"You keep saying magick," Summer said, distressed.

"Then focus on the music," the instructor said. From a distance, the small woman looked no older than Dawn. Up close, Summer could see her laugh lines and the wisdom in her eyes. "Stop thinking. Just *feel.*"

Summer couldn't do anything. The instructor winked then moved away, correcting the form of the other girls as she went. Summer stared at the clock, willing the class to be over.

It was a full hour and a half, the longest class she'd ever been in. When it ended, she was the first out the door to change into her comfortable jeans again. Summer stayed in her room until Amber came to get her.

"You holding up okay?" Amber asked, knocking as she entered.

"I don't know."

"Your next class will be a bit easier. History. You a fan of history?"

"It's okay," Summer said. The tightness in her chest unfurled a little at the thought of something so mundane.

"Come on. I'll show you to the classrooms. The bottom floor of the main house is filled with classrooms for the girls. The boys are taught in the classrooms in the dorms."

Summer went. The other girls were already in the small classroom with chairs arranged in a circle. She took the only empty chair. The instructor was another woman around Amber's age with flawless cocoa skin and hair dyed bright pink.

"You must be Summer," the instructor said with a smile. "I'm Lilian. Why don't we go around and introduce ourselves?"

Dawn started. The girls were all around Summer's age, several of them with heavy accents indicating they were from outside the country. The girl across from her blushed when she spoke and ducked her gaze, but her smile was brilliant and her accent British.

Biji, Summer repeated mentally. *From India.*

"We'll start with some basics for Summer," Lilian said. "Who can name the first Master of Light?"

"Alexander, the Lightbringer!" someone answered.

"The first Master of Dark?"

"Nataniel, the Darkbringer!"

31

"And where did they meet to create the treaty between good and evil, which we call today the Laws of Magick?"

"Priest Lake."

"How many Dark Laws are there?"

"Three."

"How many Light Laws?"

"Three."

"Who is the Mistress of Dark?"

"Rania the Firebringer."

"The Mistress of Light?"

"Nora the Silent." Another voice added, "No one's ever seen her."

"Very true," Lilian said. "She's a mysterious woman."

Summer listened, baffled. Lilian asked question after question, with the girls chiming in around her. Like this magick stuff was *real*. Summer listened, her shock fading to discomfort as the questions and discussion continued.

Magick was real. The magick within her wasn't viewed here as a curse but as a part of life. People with magick had their own school, their own history. Their own world. It sank in slowly during the one hour history lesson, until she began to believe this really wasn't some sort of dream or prank or worse— hallucination.

When they broke for the morning, Summer went to the front porch, where she could see the trees and sky. Things outside the house seemed normal compared to what she was learning inside the house. She sat on the steps, waiting to see if the figure appeared in the driveway again.

If magick was real, then so was the creature she saw. She rose and started down the driveway.

"Summer, you want to come with us swimming?" Dawn called.

She turned.

"It's supposed to be in the eighties today!"

Summer hesitated too long.

"I'll come get you in five minutes. Go put on a suit!" Dawn disappeared from the doorway.

Summer sighed and returned to her room. She didn't have a bathing suit. She had shorts and yet another ratty T-shirt she'd used the few times they'd gone swimming in the YMCA's pool. She changed into those. Dawn's five minutes stretched into an hour.

"Hey, kiddo," Amber said and opened the door. "Dawn's having some sort of crisis with her hair. I figured I'd blow your mind again while you waited."

Summer smiled despite her unease. Amber's soft, upbeat voice and cheerful smile had an effect on her. She could almost pretend the pretty woman liked her and didn't think her a freak like the other teachers always did.

"I just need this," Amber said. She sat beside Summer and plucked a hair from Summer's pillow. "Earlier, I told you about how we allow our students to choose their own paths, Light or Dark."

Summer watched. Amber carefully wound the hair around a small, clear crystal amulet. When she was done, she held it out. Summer took it, and the crystal flared to life, as if it had a Christmas light in it. The light was whiskey in color. Its magick made Summer's fingers tingle.

"This represents the magick of your soul. Everyone here has an amulet. Most wear them openly, but some prefer to hide them," Amber explained. "When you choose your path, your amulet will be claimed by either the Light or the Dark, and your soul will become one of the many that the Masters or Mistresses of Light and Dark use to generate their power.

Once the Dark path is chosen, you can never go back. Choose wisely, and remember, you will be tested."

"Like multiple choice tests?"

"No. Trials. Real-life trials. You'll never know what they are until you've been through them. There are three rules for those on the side of light to obey. One, do no harm to others. Two, help those who need it, no matter how undeserving they may be. Three, it is better to let evil win than to commit evil. Repeat them."

Summer obeyed. They seemed simple, and she'd never done anything contrary in her lifetime.

"You can use your magick as much as you'd like within those bounds."

"I don't know how," Summer admitted.

"You will learn. Now, go downstairs and wait for Dawn. I'll drag her away from the mirror."

Summer rose, the amulet in her hand. She crossed to her suitcase and pulled a simple, tarnished silver chain from her jewelry box. As she descended the stairs, she strung the amulet on it then placed it at her neck.

"Amber gave you the speech." Beck was in the living area, a beach towel slung over one arm. His smile made her body light up.

"Yes. Not sure I understand all this," Summer said. "Are you going swimming?"

"Of course."

"Oh." Summer glanced down at herself. She'd be embarrassed yet again in front of the handsome boy. She didn't even have a towel. In that moment, she decided she'd just sit this one out.

Dawn trotted down the stairs, followed by two other girls pretty enough to make Summer feel even worse. Dawn

34

wore a skimpy bikini with a thick towel over her shoulder. The other girls wore their suits, one in a bikini and the other in a one-piece that left little to the imagination. All three wore amulets around their neck.

"Van's out front, my beautiful ladies," Beck said and opened the front door with a flourish.

The three girls giggled. Summer trailed them, feeling like the ugly duckling. Beck winked at her as she passed him. A white van waited outside for them. The girls piled into the first row, leaving Summer to squeeze past them. Two other young men were in the back. She sat in her own row while Beck got into the passenger seat.

"Guys, Summer is the new girl. Summer, Adam is the one with glasses and Brandon the fool with the bad hair," Beck called back. "Jeeves, take us swimming!"

The van started forward.

Summer looked at the two guys in the back. Adam looked quiet, a tall, skinny boy with large glasses and a hesitant smile. Brandon grinned, his unruly curls covering one eye. He was built like a bowling ball, muscular and short.

She gazed out the window as they drove. Brandon and Beck bantered back and forth, with Dawn teasing Beck and the girls giggling. The forest seemed to go on forever, broken up only by dirt roads. The van turned down one dirt road, and the trip grew bumpy before they came into view of a partially paved parking lot and beyond it, a beach stretching to a murky lake.

"You swim in a lake?" Summer asked, surprised.

"It's so much better than a pool," Dawn gushed. "I guess they don't have lakes in LA. It's like the ocean, but smaller!"

Beck opened the door to the van, and the girls hopped out. Summer followed them to the last tree before the beach started then sat down beneath its shade. The girls, Beck, and Brandon all went to the water.

"You don't swim either?" Adam asked, standing in the shade beside her.

"I don't have a suit," Summer said.

"You can go out in your underwear like Dawn."

Summer laughed. Adam sat beside her in the shade. They watched the girls dip toes in the chilly lake water, squeal then try again.

"I'm from Ohio," Adam said. "We don't have pine trees."

"We don't have them in LA either," she said. "Are you in the state system, too?"

"State system? You mean like a ward of the state?"

She nodded.

"No. I have parents and two brothers. I think you're the only real live orphan here. Not that there's anything wrong with that," he added quickly. "Just that … well, I've never met an orphan before."

"We're just like most people," she said with a smile.

"That's cool. Do you miss your friends at um, orphan school?"

"I didn't really have any friends. I'm kind of different."

"Me, too. I think we all are."

"They look normal," she said, gaze on the girls frolicking in the shallows. Beck was splashing them with water.

"Yeah, they do."

She heard the same quiet loneliness in Adam's voice that she felt.

"So, do you like it here?" she asked.

"Love it. I got here last summer. I go home a few times a year for a couple weeks at a time, but mainly, I stay here. Amber is awesome, and people who have our gift of magick are welcome here. I went through so many schools that my parents were about to give up and home school me when Amber contacted them."

"I've been through a ton of schools, too," Summer said. "I hope I can make it here."

"You will. This is the place people like us are supposed to be."

She studied him, wanting to believe the place with magick in the air was the last school she'd ever be in. Adam was confident about this, if nothing else. With his hawkish nose and small eyes, he wasn't handsome, but she couldn't help thinking he was one of the most beautiful people in the world for having faith in her.

"Summer, come on!" Dawn shouted from the water.

Summer shook her head.

"Why not? It's awesome!"

Summer shook her head again.

"Oh, are you on your period?"

Summer flushed and glanced at Adam then Beck. Adam was red, too, though Beck didn't seem to have heard.

"It's ok—next week!" Dawn said.

"She likes to embarrass people," Adam said and cleared his throat.

Summer wanted to climb under a rock and stay there.

"Do you like ice cream?" Adam asked.

"Definitely."

"Come on. There's a little hot dog stand near the resort. He has ice cream bars, too." The skinny boy rose.

Grateful for the excuse to leave, Summer stood and walked with him across the sand. The beach wrapped around the curve in the lake, and a log resort came into view as they walked. It was tucked into the forest with a long dock leading out into the lake. Adam walked to the dock then up a shallow hill toward the resort. The scent of grilled hamburgers reached Summer, making her mouth water. A small outdoor seating area was populated by one family while cooks roasted a hog on a spit over one set of coals and hamburgers on another grill. Near the edge was a small cart with hotdogs and ice cream.

Adam bought them both chocolate ice cream bars. Summer took a bite and almost gagged. Like the s'more and breakfast that morning, it tasted like fish. She forced a smile at Adam when he looked at her.

"Thank you," she managed.

"I usually get one and sit on the dock. You can see all the fish."

Summer said nothing, not wanting to see fish after everything she ate tasted like it. She went with him, though. He walked about halfway down the dock then sat with his legs dangling over the edge.

"See all of them?" he asked, excited.

Summer set the ice cream down beside her then leaned over to look. Sunlight glinted off the gills of fish in the shallow, greenish water.

"I like the catfish. You shouldn't eat them, but a lot of people do," he said, pointing to one.

His face glowed. She couldn't quite relate to liking fish that much, but she was happy with his company. Adam went on to name all the fish that passed beneath them, rattling off odd facts about them.

Summer listened and laughed when he made corny fish jokes. Even if she had no interest in fish, spending the afternoon with someone as kind as Adam left her feeling content. She'd never spent any time with a boy, because she'd never been anywhere long enough to make friends.

As they walked back to the beach a couple of hours later, she began to think she really could make it in this new world. When the magick in the air and trees swirled around her, she didn't resist. Instead, she tentatively welcomed it. It swept past her then *through* her, tickling as the magick in the amulet did.

"C'mon, guys!" Beck called from the parking lot. "We're waiting!"

Summer and Adam returned to the van. It smelled of lake water. The girls were still dripping, and Dawn's gaze settled on Summer.

"Someone has a boyfriend," she whispered to her friends.

Summer pretended like she didn't hear. Adam took up his seat in the back. While she'd enjoyed her afternoon with him, she didn't feel towards him the way she did about Beck. The girls whispered as the driver took them back to the house. He dropped them off outside.

"Want to barbecue?" Beck asked as they ascended the stairs.

"Definitely!" Dawn replied.

No one else responded, and Summer hoped they didn't expect her to come. She went to her room and put on her jeans again. They were the only piece of clothing that fit her remotely well. Before anyone could seek her out, she left the house and walked down the road, towards the direction she'd seen the ape-man the evening before. She moved from the road into the forest, this time making an effort to remember her surroundings so she could find her way back.

She walked for a while. The magick of the forest drifted through her like the sun through the canopy overhead. She saw nothing out of the ordinary and heard only the songs of birds. The deeper into the forest she walked, the more she doubted her eyes. A distant sound reached her ears, and she stopped to listen.

Summer altered her direction towards the sound, expecting to frighten away whatever it was. The cry grew louder as she approached. She slowed. It sounded like the distress mewl of a young animal. Summer's heart quickened as the scent of rotting meat reached her nose. She covered it. Finally, she saw it: the lifeless, bloated body of a deer. What looked like massive claw marks had raked across its neck. Beside its body, struggling to stand at her approach, was a fawn. One of its legs was bloodied and it was too thin, as if it'd been lying beside its mother, calling for help, for days.

Real-life trial. Summer couldn't help thinking of Amber's words and the Light Laws.

The baby tried to run and collapsed on its injured leg.

"Oh, you poor thing!" Summer exclaimed. She moved forward to help it.

She reached out to stroke it, murmuring quietly. Its fur was the softest thing she'd ever felt, its dark eyes huge in the small face. It calmed some, its cries turning plaintive and hungry.

She looked at its dead mother. The fawn was an orphan like her. Touched by its plight, Summer bent over and wrapped her arms around it awkwardly, lifting it. The animal squirmed then stilled. She felt its heart racing. Summer picked her way through the forest back the way she'd come.

The skies began to grow dark as she walked, and she looked around, unable to tell her way through the forest again. The deer was quiet. By the loll of its head, it was getting weaker. She had to get it to the kitchen, where she could get milk. As dark fell, her sense of unease returned. The sounds of the forest changed with the night. The cries of birds were replaced with distant hoots of owls and rustling of animals.

She was lost. Again. Summer sat down on a tree stump to rest her arms. They ached from the effort of carrying the fawn. The small life clutched against her was slipping away. She started to panic, uncertain which way was home and if she'd get there in time. She stood, hoping to see lights from the main house through the forest.

Nothing but darkness and trees surrounded her.

"You really need to stay out of the forest."

She gasped at the familiar voice.

"Decker, is that you?"

"Who else would be out in the dark?"

"I guess anyone could be," she answered, puzzled.

There was a pause. She heard branches snap as he moved closer.

"What do you have?" he asked.

"I found a baby deer. His mother was killed. I wanted to take him back to the house, but I got lost again."

"You can't have pets."

"He's not a pet!" she replied. "He's hurt. I just want to help him get better."

"If I take you back again, will you promise to stay out of the forest at night?"

"Yes, of course."

"You need help carrying it?" He sounded irritated, as if he had something better to do in the forest after dark than lead her around.

"Um, no," she lied, afraid to tell him her arms were shaking already.

She felt the warmth of his body heat as he approached. His hands brushed her arm as he took the small beast from her. His magick flew through her, startling her. It was warm and cool at once, the sensations sizzling along her nerve endings. The world around her felt more alive, the night darker, the breeze cooler.

"Come on then," he directed, unaffected by the brush of their hands.

The sensations left her. She hurried to follow him, afraid of being left in the forest. Decker walked for half an hour before breaking out onto the road leading to the house. Summer expected him to pass off the deer to her then disappear. He kept walking until he reached the house then around the side, opening a side door that led directly into the quiet kitchen. Summer lingered in the doorway, unable to see. The lights flipped on, and Decker strode out.

Her eyes went to the fawn on the island in the middle. It looked so small and weak. It wasn't moving. She rushed to it, petting its soft fur. It was warm. She touched the wound on his leg.

Summer went to the fridge and pulled out a gallon of milk then gazed around. She didn't have a bottle or anything to use to feed it. She'd seen one of the teens at the orphanage use a turkey baster instead when she lost the bottle for her infant. Summer began to open the drawers of the kitchen, looking for one.

"We'll have to clean its wound."

Summer looked up, surprised that Decker returned. He carried rags and an armful of other things. He set them down, and she saw the rubbing alcohol, topical ointment, and bandages. He set to work carefully cleaning the small animal's leg while she found the turkey baster. She microwaved a glass of milk then filled the baster.

"That's a good idea," Decker said, glancing at the turkey baster when she returned to the island. "It's a bite. Doesn't look infected, which is lucky."

She watched him wrap the deer's leg in a bandage. The deer had awoken and lay still.

"Poor thing," she murmured, stroking its face. "I wonder if he'll survive."

"I don't know. He's pretty beat up."

Summer's heart broke for the baby. To survive an attack that killed its mother, only to die here, when it had a chance … the deer was like her. She had a second chance; the deer would, too. Resolve settled into her. She picked up her new ward.

"He'll make it," she said. "I'll take care of him." She walked to the door.

"Remember, stay out of the forest after dark," Decker called after her. "I'm serious this time."

Summer hesitated at the door, facing him. His dark eyes were on her. He wore all black, as usual, and his arms were crossed. Her body tingled in memory of their brief touch, and she couldn't help the warmth that rose to her face.

"I will. Thank you, Decker," she said.

"No problem, Summer."

The way he said her name and held her gaze made her want to linger. She didn't know what it was, but being around him made the air between them sizzle. Summer turned away and went to her room. She set the deer down on her bed and locked her door before trying to feed the animal. It resisted at first then drank a little before refusing. Summer pulled pillows from her roommate's bed and built a fort around her fawn to keep him from rolling off the bed in the middle of the night.

She took a quick shower then lay down on the edge of the bed, wrapping her body around the side of the fawn that the pillow fort didn't cover. Worried, she drifted into a restless sleep.

Chapter Four

DECKER STOOD IN the kitchen for a long minute, unable to register what he'd felt when their hands brushed. The sense they were connected grew stronger with their touch. His hand tingled from where it grazed her arm, and he tried to shake the sensation off.

"You're not supposed to be in the house after eight," Amber said, walking into the kitchen. "No guys in the girls' dorm."

"I know."

"You wouldn't by chance have seen Summer? She wasn't at dinner today." There was worry on Amber's face. She was one of the few people he could tolerate for more than a few minutes. Her soul always sang happily, rendering her presence almost as soothing as Sam's.

"She's fine. She got lost in the forest," he replied. "I found her and brought her back."

"Oh, good." Amber relaxed visibly. She crossed to the refrigerator. "You want something to eat?"

"No. Beck and I are going to visit our parents. We'll be back by breakfast."

Amber pursed her lips at him, but she didn't lecture him about the rule of not leaving the grounds after dark. After all, his father owned the refuge for witchlings. He was the one person who could change the rules if he wanted.

"You okay, sweetie?" she asked, studying him. "I can't imagine anything in the forest would scare you, but you look like something did."

"I'm fine," Decker said. "Not scared. Just … you know. Dreading my birthday."

"I can't imagine."

"Yeah."

She held his gaze and gave him a smile of encouragement. Decker didn't think there was anything anyone in the world could do to help him once he turned eighteen. Amber seemed to know that as well, for her expression turned pitying. She said nothing.

Decker walked out. There was nothing she could say, but he almost wished she'd tried to tell him it wouldn't be that bad. Not that he'd believe her, just that he'd appreciate her concern.

The shuttle van was waiting for him, the side door yawning open. Beck had claimed the passenger seat and was talking with the driver, an older man who'd retired from teaching at the school a year before. Decker climbed in and slammed the door shut.

The shuttle took them to their parents' lakeside cabin, near the resort. The house was brighter than a pine tree at Christmas. Grayish smoke curled from the massive chimney. They left the shuttle driver and entered through the open garage, emerging into a kitchen bursting with the scents of home-cooked food. Their grandfather—who acted as their parents' personal chef— was finishing up prepping small meals and freezing them, something he did for the boys he'd helped raise. He was a small, Native American man with white hair and wise eyes.

"Louis!" Beck said with a grin. "I love you, man!"

"You are very welcome," Louis said. He grunted as Beck hugged him, his stern features softening.

"Hey, Grandpa Louis," Decker said, smiling. "I see you survived yet another trip."

"I hate flying," Louis replied. "But someone's got to take care of your parents."

The more outgoing of the twins, Beck stayed to chat while Decker moved to where he knew his mother would be: in the family room. He sensed her, the way he sensed anyone with Dark magick. Hers rolled off of her in warm-cool waves that enveloped him like perfume long before he reached the family room. His parents sat there, waiting for them.

"Hello, son," his mother said in her velvety voice. She flipped through a magazine and didn't look up to see which twin entered.

"Mother," Decker said. "Hello, Father."

"Good to see you, Decker."

His father smiled and stood to give him a brief embrace. Middle-aged with graying hair, the noble features of their ancestral Native American tribe, and a lean frame, Michael Turner looked less like the billionaire entrepreneur he was and more like a newscaster. He wore jeans and a sports jacket, though his feet were bare. His soul was like that of Amber's: soothing and happy.

Decker didn't look at his mother, the Mistress of Fire and Night, until he sat down in one of the chairs near the fireplace. Rania glanced up at him then, her beauty and darkness mesmerizing even to him. With long hair and large brown eyes, she looked almost twenty years younger than her age. Her clothing— while meticulous and expensive— was always tight, revealing her toned shape and long legs. This night, she wore a velvet, one-piece jumpsuit that made her look like a panther crouched on the couch. Her aura was as dark as her black hair. Even he felt the threat in her gaze, the one that reminded him she'd claimed her own son's soul the night he fell from the path of Light.

"Mom! Pop!" Beck called cheerfully as he entered. He hugged both parents, unaffected by their mother's darkness. "We thought you were in Europe all summer."

"We're going back tomorrow," their father said. "This trip will cause us to miss your birthdays, so we thought it was important to see you before then."

"It's a big day for both of you," Rania said. "We talked about it and decided we'll lift your suspended privileges on your birthday."

"Yes!" Beck exclaimed. "I'm so sick of walking everywhere."

"Happy Birthday," Michael said with a laugh. "Just kidding. We got you both something else and hid it in the house. We'll text you on your birthday with the secret location."

"We're not ten anymore, Dad," Decker said, smiling. "You don't have to hide our birthday and Christmas presents."

"We're too old for a treasure hunt," Beck agreed.

"The first clue is in the fridge," their father said, ignoring them.

Decker met Beck's gaze. They were still for a moment then dashed simultaneously towards the kitchen. Decker shoved Beck into a wall then landed flat on his stomach when Beck tripped him. The chef scurried out of their paths as they reached the fridge, both jostling to be the first to open it.

Decker wrenched open the fridge door. Both stared into the neatly kept space, seeking anything out of place among the stacked containers, fresh food, and dairy items.

"I believe you'll find what you seek in the butter drawer," Louis said from a few feet away, amused.

Beck ducked beneath Decker's arm and opened the butter drawer. In it were two sets of keys, one with a blue tag and the other black. Beck handed Decker the black tag. They were quiet as they looked at the tag.

"BMW," Beck said.

"Harley," Decker said.

They grinned at each other and retreated to the family room. Their father was waiting with a smile.

"Perfect," Decker said first. "I didn't see anything in the garage."

"They'll appear like magick on your birthday," Michael said with a wink. "Both are customized. And both contain GPSs with speed monitors. If you go over seventy miles an hour, I get a text alert. Brilliant, isn't it?"

"Really?" Beck demanded. "When we're eighteen, we can do what we want."

"Then go buy your own car, son," their mother, Rania, purred.

Beck rolled his eyes, but Decker smiled. He had one thing to look forward to. Knowing their father, the vehicles would be top of the line, in the boys' favorite colors.

"Thanks," he said, pleased.

His suspension from motorcycles had prevented him from escaping when the sounds of others' souls got too loud at the school. His only reprieve was hiding in the forest. In a few weeks, he could leave again, drown out the sounds of humanity with the roar of a Harley and the wind. The idea made him feel at ease for the first time in a long time.

"Now that you've got the carrot, it's time for the stick," their mother said, standing. "Your life will change when you turn eighteen. We postponed your vision quests until you assumed your new roles. When we're back from Europe in Fall, your father will take you out for your official *weyekin* ceremonies. But tonight, you're going on a different kind of rite of passage. I want you both to see what it will mean for you to turn eighteen, so you appreciate your family and your heritage a little more."

Decker pocketed the keys, sensing how serious she was. Beck mirrored his movement.

"You're going on a field trip," their father said. "It's not meant to scare you. But we wanted both of you to have an idea of what Decker will be going through."

"My own twin abandoned me on our eighteenth birthdays. Your father and I swore we wouldn't let the same happen to you," Rania said. The sadness that trickled into her voice whenever she spoke of her estranged twin, Nora—the Mistress of Light—was present. "You will not abandon each other."

"Decker's a jackass, but I won't abandon him," Beck replied.

50

"The transition is not an easy one," their mother said, gazing at Decker.

Decker's chest tightened. He didn't know what she wanted to show them, but it wouldn't be pleasant.

"I'm ready for it, Mother," he said with more confidence than he felt.

"No one is ever ready for it," she said, not unkindly. "Come with me, my boys. Let me show you my world."

She held out her hands ,and Beck took one. Decker took the other, and cold and fire tore through him, taking his breath. Their surroundings changed suddenly from the cozy family room to a dark alley. Wherever they were, it was rainy and cold. The buildings on either side were made of weather-worn stone, resembling the ancient structures that still made up some of the small towns in northern Europe. They spent every summer exploring the European landscape.

"Ouch," Beck said when he could breathe again.

"Hush. Follow me," Rania said, unaffected by the chill in the air around them.

Decker glanced towards his twin in the night and stepped after his mother. She led him down the alley and onto a quiet street lined with streetlamps. His mother moved as quietly as a shadow. He shivered in the cold, wet air, wishing she'd let them grab their jackets before taking them.

His mother approached a darkened storefront, passed it, and opened the door to the side leading up to a second floor with flats. Beck motioned to the door as he followed, indicating the lock she'd somehow bypassed effortlessly. Decker closed the door behind him, and they both confirmed it locked.

"We have to ask her how to do that," Beck whispered as they ascended after their shadowy mother. She disappeared around the corner at the top of the stairwell.

Decker hurried to catch up. The water-stained drywall of the second floor smelled heavily of mold, and a television blared behind one of the doors lining the narrow hallway.

His mother seemed to know exactly where she went. She waved for them to keep up as she stopped outside a door then opened it. It closed behind her. Decker reached it too late to grab it and twisted the knob. It was locked.

"So weird," Decker mumbled. "I thought she walked through walls."

"I guess she doesn't have to. This is how she kept getting my porno stash last summer," Beck grumbled. "I had it behind lock and key."

"*Our* porno stash. I told you to give it to Grandpa Louis. She leaves him alone."

The door swung open, startling both of them. Their mother raised her eyebrow at them and motioned them to follow again. She disappeared into the darkness beyond.

Heart pounding hard, Decker went in first. He had no idea what to expect. He saw the lumpy outlines of furniture in the apartment. He heard his mother open another door without seeing her and moved towards the sound. He tripped over a rug then smacked his leg into something hard that shouldn't have been in the middle of the apartment in the first place.

"Watch your step," he whispered to Beck. His warning came too late, and he heard Beck make the same mistakes.

"God *damn* it!" Beck muttered.

Decker waited another minute until his eyes adjusted to continue. He stepped cautiously in the direction his mother had gone. She'd had no problem navigating the flat. He tripped once more then made it to the doorway where she waited for them. He didn't see her until he'd almost run into her.

"Come on, boys," she said.

The room she stepped into was small and dark, lit by light outlining a cracked doorway on one side and filtering through the curtains on the other side. Decker guessed it was a bedroom by the rough size and shape of a bed to his right.

"Wait right here," Rania said. His mother strode straight to the bathroom door and pushed it open.

A gunshot went off, and Decker cursed loudly at the roaring sound in the silent apartment. Another one went off. Beck grabbed his arm, pointing to the bed. Decker glanced at what the light of the bathroom revealed then hurried forward, more concerned about his mother being shot.

"Come in, boys!" she called as he reached the doorway. Beck crowded behind him.

Decker stared. His mother crouched in front of a man with white-blond hair who sat on the floor of a bathroom that reeked of vomit. She held the gun and set it on the counter, out of the man's reach.

"This is Istvan. He's been skirting me for a while." Her voice was a low, calm purr.

The man's terrified eyes went from her to Decker. The man called Istvan was shaking and silent.

"If you saw the body on the bed, you'll know Istvan snapped finally. Decker." She twisted to meet his gaze. "When someone from the Light falls, you feel it. It's like someone slaps you awake in the morning. You can feel him, what he's done, which Laws he's broken. You can also find him, anywhere he runs. Eventually, you will find him." She returned her attention to the cowering man. "Not that you didn't try to evade me, Istvan. But this has gone on long enough."

"He killed someone," Beck said in a hushed voice.

"He killed a lot of people. But only two directly. It's one thing to use magick to kill and another to use magick to set the stage for someone dying. This isn't the first time he lost control."

"You mean you knew and let him go before?" Decker asked.

"I knew what he was long before his first kill but couldn't act. This is the true burden, son," she said. "Either knowing someone should be stripped of his Light. Or, knowing someone who was did not deserve it. In either case, you are bound by duty to claim the soul. In Istvan's case, he somehow managed to avoid me even after he crossed that line."

At her words, the man named Istvan began to weep. He struggled to his feet. Rania rose with him and took a step back while Decker and Beck crammed themselves into the bathroom to protect her, if needed.

Istvan tried to shove past their mother. A flash of darkness filled the bathroom then cleared just as suddenly. Their mother glowed with seething evil. It drank the white of her eyes and moved through and around her body. She slammed Istvan to the ceiling with her power, pinning him there. His amulet dangled over her head.

"For breaking the Light Laws, you are condemned." Her voice took on an inhuman note. "Your soul is my food, your Light my drink. Your soul is now lost forever."

Istvan's tears fell from the ceiling. She took his amulet and studied it. With a frown, she unwrapped one long, black hair—that resembled hers more than the blond Istvan's—from the amulet then dropped the trinket to the ground, smashing it with her heel. The white light within swirled around her leg. Her shadows swallowed it and she sighed, as if deeply satisfied. The amulet reformed itself, glowing black.

"Our power comes from those who are damned." Her voice slowly returned to normal. "We feed on them, Decker. It sustains us. When one sins, we become thirsty and hungry, until we claim them."

Decker's mouth was too dry to respond. He remembered when she'd claimed his soul. She'd been gentle, taking his amulet and returning when it was black while he sobbed in his room.

Don't worry, she'd assured him. *You are the next Master of Fire and Night. When others die, their souls are lost forever. Yours will not be, for you are a servant of Light and Dark.*

This man's soul was lost forever.

Beck's breathing was ragged in Decker's ears.

"What happens if you don't claim him?" Beck asked.

"I forfeit my own soul." Their mother faced them, her eyes still black. They stepped back in unison, away from her.

"I don't know if I can do this," Decker whispered.

"You must," she said. She held out her hands to them.

Decker hesitated before taking one while Beck took the other. More fire shot through them, and they were somewhere else, in a forest. At once, Decker recognized the feel of the forest near the school and relaxed.

"That's it? What about the woman?" Beck asked. "You didn't even call the police."

"That's not what I do," their mother said gently. "I am there for one purpose only. To enforce the Law of Magick."

Decker sat on the ground, lightheaded. Beck gripped his shoulder.

55

"Mother, how can you make Decker do this?" his twin demanded.

"It must be done, Beck. Would you rather that guy wander the streets, using his magick to kill?"

"What will make him stop?" Decker asked. "You took his soul. But he's still alive. I'm still alive."

"You can't compare people like us to them," she warned. "We are born into our positions and expected to perform evil in the name of good. Once a soul is lost, it can never be recovered. The souls of those who do good return to the world even after the witchling dies and becomes a part of nature. The souls of those who do evil must be destroyed, or they will continue to do evil even in death."

"But he can still do evil now," Beck insisted. "You've done nothing to protect innocent people from him!"

"That becomes your role, Beck. Decker will enforce. You will protect. Decker is not the only one who can kill those who go astray. The role has fallen solely to me over the past twenty years, because of my twin sister's rather absent dedication to her duties."

They were silent.

"Worst practical example ever," Decker said at last. "Who enforces those Dark witchlings who become threats to everyone? I mean, there are layers in evil, right?"

"That's our next stop," Rania said. "Those who break the Laws of Magick become Dark. Those who break the Dark Laws are killed."

"You kill them?" Beck asked in a strangled voice.

"I do. We have three Dark Laws. No magick involving the dead. Second, no evil can be stolen from a witchling by another witchling. Third, evil wasted weakens us all. This is a catch-all. I can use it to kill anyone I feel uses their magick inappropriately. It's meant to give the Dark Master or Mistress more freedom than the Light Master has. Beck can only kill when absolutely necessary."

Decker closed his eyes as she spoke. He felt sick.

"The next man we visit broke the third law. Magick is finite, and he's used his to the point of madness."

"I'm not sure I want to see this." Beck voiced the words Decker wanted to say.

"You will, though, Beck. My sister left me to deal with my power alone. I won't see that happen to Decker, not when the two of you need each other," their mother said firmly. "Light and Dark need one another. Only when the enforcer and protector work together can they truly make a difference. My split with Nora severed our effectiveness, too, and altered the balance between Light and Dark. The result is a world with more evil and death than there should be. The pendulum will continue to swing in my direction, if you two do not work together to bring balance back."

"But isn't that what we want?" Decker asked. "Shouldn't I want a world with more evil and Beck want a world with more good?"

"Evil cannot be stopped, only contained. By serving the Dark, we become a part of it. We monitor and enforce its laws from within. We don't do it so that evil can prevail but so that it doesn't take over," she explained.

"We're fighting for the same thing but in different ways," Beck said.

"And hated by everyone," Decker added.

"Yes, son, this is true." The sadness was in his mother's voice again. "You will be very alone. I met your father when I was seventeen, and we married when I was twenty. I was twenty-five when you were born. He's been my sanity, and you

57

both have been my whole world. Even so, keeping the secret of what you are from those you love most is very difficult."

The revulsion Decker felt watching her do what she did faded at her words. He couldn't quite come to grips with knowing she'd done this her whole adult life and protected them both from it until tonight. But he pitied her and himself for taking on a duty that made him want to vomit.

"It's for the good of everyone," his mother added, as if aware of his thoughts. "And it's only until your children turn eighteen, Decker."

Decker drew a deep breath. He didn't want to say what was on his mind, that he didn't think he'd cope well enough being a soul reaper to date anytime soon. Or ever.

"Not really a romantic introduction," Beck joked weakly. "Hi, I'm Decker. I'll take your soul if you screw up."

"You take souls, too," Decker pointed out.

"*Good* souls. It's like comparing a candy bar and a stick of dynamite. If I remember correctly, killing is how you got sentenced to the Dark."

"Lame." Decker snorted. "You would've done the same if you were there."

As they bantered, their mother withdrew the long, dark hair she'd pulled off of Istvan's amulet. Frowning, she held it up in the moonlight. Decker was about to ask her about it when she shook her head. She replaced the hair in her pocket then leveled her dark gaze on him.

"You guys sound like you've recovered. Come on," she said. "You've gotta be back at the school before dawn."

Heart beating faster than a hummingbird's wings, Decker stood, knowing he wasn't anywhere near ready to see his mother kill someone.

Chapter Five

"SUMMER, AREN'T YOU hungry?"

Summer looked from her plate to Dawn, who sat down the table from her at breakfast. There were a few kids up already, including the Turner twins, both of whom appeared half-asleep at the other end of the table.

"Not too much," Summer replied. She pushed her nearly full plate away.

She was *starving*. But everything here tasted like fish after the first night. She didn't understand it.

"You need to eat. You're skin and boobs," Dawn said with a laugh. The girls flanking her laughed as well.

Summer's face grew hot. She rose and returned to her room, where the small deer still slept in the middle of its pillow fortress. She patted its head then left the room quietly.

"I was just coming to get you for dance class," Amber said from down the hall. "You ready?"

Summer nodded. They descended to the first floor and down the hallway to the dance studio. Everyone was already there. She took up her place in the back of the class, mind on the deer in her room. She went through the motions the instructor showed them. Before she could flee back to her room, Amber stopped her.

"The rest of the girls have the day off. You and I are going to do some introductory magick studies. Meet me out back in half an hour? Is that enough time for you to change?"

Summer nodded and ran back to her room.

Her deer still slept. She hovered over it for a few minutes before changing into jeans. She'd grabbed some milk at breakfast; it sat on her dresser, waiting for her friend to awaken. It didn't during her short break, and she left it grudgingly.

Amber waited for her at one of the picnic tables. In front of her, outlined by rocks and candles, was a circle around a pentagram. She patted the table beside her, and Summer sat.

"You look a little pale," Amber said, studying her. "Are you sleeping well?"

"Well enough," Summer said. "I don't like the food here."

"Seriously? You seemed okay with it the first night."

Summer shrugged. She didn't know why, either.

"Wait a minute." Amber hopped off the table and drew a crystal and some sage from the bag between them. She lit the sage, tied the crystal to its base, and blew on the fiery herb until smoke puffed towards Summer. The rich, earthy scent was comforting.

Amber murmured a few words as she waved the sage around Summer. She motioned for her to stand, and

Summer did, watching her teacher circle her with the smoking herb.

"That should take care of it," Amber said. "Lesson one. When you use magick, and there's any left over, burn it to return it to nature."

She tossed the sage into the center of the pentagram.

The sound of a car door closing drew Summer's attention towards the house. A tall woman with black hair and wearing a suit entered the side door leading into the kitchen.

"That's Matilda," Amber said quietly. "You remember how I told you I teach the children of the Light?"

Amber nodded.

"She teaches the children of the Dark."

Summer's gaze lingered on the door. The woman seemed the opposite of Amber, even from a distance. Her hair was short and kept in place by hairspray, her slender figure clad in formal wear. Amber floated over the ground in her skirts; Matilda marched.

"Okay, now we need to figure out what element is yours."

Summer looked at Amber.

"Do you have any idea?" Amber asked. "Do you feel drawn to anything? Fire? Water?"

"I don't know about drawn," Summer replied slowly. "But there's like, this tingling I get from the wind and the forest."

"Very good. You may have a primary and secondary element. Can you tell which is stronger?"

"No."

"Which did you feel first when you arrived?"

"Probably the wind. It tried to flip up my shirt," Summer said.

"Then we'll go with air primary and earth secondary." Amber smiled. "This is very good. Few students have a secondary. It must make the forest feel very comfortable to you."

"It does, except at night."

"A reminder of our rules. You shouldn't be out in the forest at night."

"I got lost."

"Now that you know your element, all you have to do is ask it for directions."

Summer almost laughed at the ridiculous thought of asking the wind for directions, until she saw Amber wasn't joking.

"Your element might've been trying to warn you, too," Amber added.

She retrieved her bag and dug around in it. She pulled out a turquoise cabochon the size of Summer's thumb and handed it to her. The stone hummed with magick in Summer's hand.

"This is for your primary element. It'll help you communicate with the air."

Amber dug out a piece of green jade in the shape of a small elephant. Summer smiled as she looked at its intricately carved features.

"This one is for the earth."

The buzz from this one was weaker in her hand. She placed them both in one hand, fascinated by the sensations running through her palm and up her forearm.

"Every student learns a different way to communicate with their elements," Amber continued.

"Do Dark students have elements?"

"They do. Our magickks and theirs are all based off the five elements. They have simply chosen to use them outside the three rules that guide the Light."

"If there's a Dark teacher here, are there Dark students?"

"The children in black."

She looked up. "They're ... evil?"

"They've chosen to use their gifts outside of our three rules," Amber said. "They are governed by their own three rules, ones you'll never know, so long as you stay within ours."

"Even Decker?"

"Yes."

Summer frowned. She'd felt something deep last night when Decker touched her, like his body awoke hers. How could he be *evil*?

"But why are they here then? Shouldn't they keep away from us?" she demanded.

"This is where the balance of good and evil is struck," Amber replied patiently. "You cannot have a balance without both, now can you?"

"No, but if they're evil, how ..." Summer didn't know what to ask.

"They're not evil, Summer. They made choices that fall outside ours. That doesn't mean they don't also keep to some of our rules. Most do no harm, but most have also chosen to use their powers for selfish reasons, and not for reasons that help another or protect another," Amber explained.

"It seems so harsh to call them bad when they might have made a mistake."

"Perhaps. But that is how good and evil work. Our rules are very simple. They're about selflessness. Would you ever knowingly hurt someone?"

"No, of course not."

"Would you ever knowingly not help someone in need?"

"No," Summer said, mind on her deer.

"Would you do evil?"

"No."

"It's that simple. The path is at your feet already."

Summer didn't think it was simple at all, but she said nothing. She concentrated on what Amber told her as much as she could while her thoughts kept going to her deer. That night at dinner, she found her taste buds had improved, and she ate as she had her first night there, relishing the taste of food.

Decker hadn't been able to sleep in three nights, since the night with their mother. He lay awake in the dorm. By Beck's tossing and turning, his twin couldn't sleep either. Fed up waiting, he rose and pulled on his jeans and a sweatshirt.

"I'm grabbing some food. You want anything?" he asked.

"Cookies," Beck said.

"Be back in a few."

Decker stepped into the cool night and gazed up at the moon and clear skies. The square was silent, the scents of the evening barbecue still in the air. Stuffing his hands into his pockets, he walked to the kitchen and turned on the light.

The small form in the open door of the fridge straightened, startled. If he wasn't so preoccupied, he would've sensed her. Summer faced him, eyes large and a gallon of milk clutched in her hands. She seemed relieved it was him and closed the door.

"My fawn needs some food," she said.

"I came for cookies," he said.

64

"There are cookies here?"

"In the cabinet." He lifted his chin towards the cupboards behind her.

She turned and set the milk on the counter then opened the cabinet. The cookies were on a plate on the top shelf, beyond her reach. Decker crossed to her and stretched over her to get them. His body brushed hers again, sending a jolt of magick through him. It was even stronger this time than the first. Summer hunched away and twisted to face him, glancing up.

The awkward lack of space between them made his body warm. Her dark eyes were soft, her scent earthy. He stepped away, unable to shake the strange effect she had on him. He pretended he didn't notice the tension between them and set the cookies on the table.

"You want to join me?" he asked, expecting her to decline.

"Yes."

He glanced up, and their gazes locked again. The sense of a shared fate returned to him. Someone who glowed with goodness could never understand what he'd soon be forced to do. Watching his mother take another's life had made him vomit, and he was Dark. Summer was too good to share a fate with him.

Decker looked away finally and sat at the breakfast bar. She sat two stools over and reached for a cookie.

"I love cookies," she said. "And most food."

"I can only eat cookies during the off season."

"What sport do you play?"

"Swimming."

"Do you swim in the lake here?" she asked.

"Yep. I've swum across it a few times."

"It looks dirty." Her nose crinkled.

Decker studied her, sensing her magick. It was still locked, as was every witchling's power until they learned to control it. It was harder to read when trapped in her body.

"You're air and earth?" he asked.

"Yes."

"You don't like water at all then," he guessed.

"Not to swim in, no. I love the ocean from a distance."

"I feel like I'm in my natural element in the water."

"I do when …" She tilted her head to the side. "I think when I'm in the forest is best for me. I'm still trying to understand all this, uh, magick stuff."

"It takes awhile," he replied and bit into a chocolate chip cookie.

Summer looked distressed rather than assured by his words. Her soul sang a sad song. She nibbled on a cookie, gaze distant. He wondered what could upset someone so sweet that she'd rescue a deer in the middle of the forest. She'd been exhausted but determined when he found her that night, the fawn trembling in her shaking arms. The pretty girl had a good heart, even if her soul was sad.

"I don't really fit in anywhere I go. So I hope I have awhile," she said at last.

"I don't fit in either."

"I can see that." Her words were accompanied by a small smile. "I burnt down one of my schools by accident once."

He choked back a laugh. Summer flushed in embarrassment.

"That's awesome," he said. "I've never done that."

"Bad stuff happens around me. I hope I can stay here, though."

"Amber will help you. She's a good person," he assured her. "If you make something explode here, we have the power to stop it."

"Dark power," she murmured. She gazed at him intently for a moment then shook her head. "You don't seem evil, Decker."

"I'm not."

She didn't look convinced and reached for another cookie.

Irritated, he wanted to throw the plate of cookies against a wall and leave. She was reacting to him the same way everyone did. But something about her and their strange connection made him stay despite the reaction he loathed. Being with her almost made him forget the look in the eyes of the man his mother killed.

"I know I can't go in the forest after dark, but it seems like it'd be beautiful," she said.

Decker sneaked a glance at her. Her gaze was on her cookie. He relaxed some to see she wasn't getting ready to flee the kitchen to escape from him.

"It's very beautiful," he said. "But you can't go."

"I know." She rolled her eyes at him. "No one will really tell me why, either. I want to see the stars. We couldn't see them in LA because of the light pollution."

"You can see the stars if you lay on one of the picnic tables in the Square," he said.

"Am I allowed out back at night?"

"Yeah. Come on." He grabbed a handful of cookies and rose. "There's one picnic table where the trees don't block everything."

Summer followed him, the gallon of milk forgotten. She stopped when she exited, and he looked over his shoulder at her. Her dark gaze was on him. While he didn't glow as dark as his mother, he knew the night only enhanced the shadows around him. He kept walking, expecting her to leave and disappointed at the thought she'd be as frightened of him as most girls were.

"This is the one," he said and paused at a table. To his surprise, she'd followed. She climbed onto the table, unafraid. Her eyes on the sky, Summer stretched back on the table until she was lying on it.

"You're right," she whispered. "This is perfect."

Decker considered returning to his room but stopped, enjoying her company. He sat and lay on one of the hard, wood benches, leaving the table top to her. He didn't need to touch her to feel their connection, but he wished he could. The sensations were more intense then.

"What's your favorite constellation?" she asked.

"I don't think I have a favorite. You?"

"Orion. He owns the sky whenever he's there. He's the opposite of me."

"If you're blowing up schools, it sounds like you're leaving an impression, too."

Her soft laughter made him smile. The sad song of her soul turned, and he closed his eyes, listening. The sounds joined the distant gurgle of his water magick and the soothing crackle of his fire magick. The combination relaxed him, made him feel drowsy for the first time in days.

"Do you like it here so far?" he asked.

"I do. It's different. All the talk about magick weirds me out, but I'm understanding more every day."

"It doesn't help that they don't give you a book explaining everything when you arrive."

"No, it really doesn't. Did you have trouble understanding everything?"

"Not until I crossed to the Dark."

Summer fell silent.

"How is your deer?" he asked, not wanting to scare her off.

"Not as good as I hoped. Not sure he'll make it."

"He will. Don't give up on him. Sometimes the most broken are the ones in the most need of a second chance."

Summer's face appeared over the edge of the table, blocking his view of the sky. She gazed down at him. Her skin was like porcelain in the moonlight, her plump lips too close for his comfort. He hadn't been able to date anyone seriously since falling from the Light. Her intent look and the nearness of her blooming body stirred his blood, reminding him of the other sensation he felt around her he'd been trying to ignore.

"Do you feel broken?" she asked.

"Yeah."

"So do I."

"You're not," he replied, bothered by her response. "I don't even know you, but I know that."

"Just like I know you are," she murmured.

"I'm probably not the guy you should be sitting with outside after dark," he agreed, agitated at the reminder.

"Don't be mad. I didn't mean anything by it."

"It's okay. I'm used to it."

Summer's features softened into another of her magickal smiles. She looked beautiful in the moonlight, gazing at him. Decker let himself think about what it would be like to have a girlfriend, one as sweet and fun to talk to as this one, who wouldn't judge him for what he was. He found himself reaching up to touch her and stopped himself.

Even if someone like Summer accepted him, he couldn't draw her into his world. It was too dark for her. In a few weeks, he'd spend his nights hunting down those who broke

Dark Laws and killing those who couldn't be salvaged. She'd turn on him, as had everyone else in the school when he crossed over to the Dark. Her magickal smile would fade, and she'd revile what he was.

"I gotta go," he mumbled and sat up.

Rising, he didn't look back, even when her soul's song turned sad once again. The idea he caused it made him grit his teeth. She deserved better. No woman deserved to be with him. His mother had met his father long before she turned Dark. He had no partner; he never would.

Returning to his dorm room, he closed the door and leaned against it, the clamor back in his thoughts. Beck's breathing was deep, and he didn't stir at Decker's entrance. He pushed himself away from the door and set a few cookies on Beck's nightstand before pulling on hiking boots.

He waited until Summer was gone from the Square before he left the school grounds for the forest. He walked through the woods until he sensed what he sought, the telltale signs of Dark magick being practiced. Decker followed the earthy scent of burning herbs, reaching a small meadow. Three other Dark students were at the center of the meadow, one standing within the pentagram they'd made out of rocks while the others flanked him outside the circle.

Incense candles burned in waist-high tiki torches at each of the pentagram's points. He recognized the scent of blood as well; they'd sacrificed animals to curry the favor of otherworldly demons on earth. He remained in the shadows, listening to the quiet chants as magick swept around the three. The form in the center knelt as the candles burned low and bowed his head. The other two stepped back. Decker approached then.

"Hey, Decker," one of them, a girl a year older than him, greeted him. "Kenny's in mourning."

"What happened?" he asked.

"I guess someone attacked his little brother. Put him in the hospital. The wind told him who it was, so he's offered blood for a demon to seek revenge," Alexa said.

"Isn't his brother like, five?" Decker asked with a frown.

"Yeah. Cute little guy. They don't think he'll make it."

"I'd kill anyone who hurt Beck, too." *Even though he gets on my nerves.* Decker watched as the shadows of the night took a fuzzy shape and approached the teen in the center of the pentagram.

Watching his mother the other night had made him feel as if he didn't belong to Light or Dark. Yet the thought of someone hurting a child and getting away with it made him realize his personality was better suited to the Dark, where he could do something about it, than in the Light, where they were forced to turn the other cheek.

"Hey, I was wondering if you'd want to go to the mall with me sometime?" Alexa's tone turned warmer as she looked up at him. "I've got a car. We can hang out."

"Probably not," he said, mind on Sam's warnings. He had to stay close to his brother and the new girl, even if staying close to the school made his head hurt.

"Oh. Well, you want to hang out here together?"

Decker glanced down at Alexa. A pretty brunette, she had one more year at the school until she'd be free to go at the age of twenty. Her nose piercing glimmered in the moonlight, and shadows kept him from seeing her bright blue eyes. He thought of the frustrated desire he'd felt for Summer. His body grew warm at the thought of her. He couldn't have her, but every other Dark girl hit on him from time to time. He could have *someone*.

"Sure," he said.

"Great!" Alexa replied. "We can hang out tomorrow?"

"Yeah, sounds fine."

She smiled, not noticing his lukewarm response. Decker watched the shadow demon listen to the teen in the center of the pentagram. It faded into the darkness when it was done. Alexa and the other girl returned to their positions to finish the ceremony. Decker watched Alexa. She was a runner with a slender body.

He felt nothing towards her, though, not even the stirring of desire. But he had to get his mind off the strange connection with Summer, before he got both of them in trouble. Before his eighteenth birthday and she turned on him.

He wandered the forest until dawn, skipped breakfast, and returned to his dorm room for a shower. Beck was there. The two looked at each other. Their strained relationship had turned tense after their field trip with their mother.

"Thanks for the cookies." Beck broke the silence.

"No problem."

"Where were you?"

"Forest."

"Alone?"

"Yeah."

"Alexa came looking for you."

Decker said nothing and peeled off his shirt, tossing it in a laundry basket in the corner.

"So … what?" Beck prompted. "You're seeing someone now?"

"Does it matter?" Decker snapped.

"Yeah."

Decker glanced at Beck. His Light twin didn't look like he was trying to pick a fight. His hands were at his side, his stance open. If anything, he looked concerned.

"I'm not dating her. I get lonely. It's no big deal," Decker said with a shrug.

"I'm not trying to be a dick. She gives me the creeps is all. You can do better."

"Someone like Dawn?"

"Look, I'm just being a good brother," Beck replied. "You have a hard enough path ahead of you without the drama of someone like that."

"Thanks," Decker said noncommittally. "I'm not looking for anything long term with anyone."

"Then you chose the right girl. From what I hear, she sleeps around on both sides."

Decker shrugged. Beck rolled his eyes and shook his head. After a shower, Decker barely had time to get dressed before someone knocked at his door. He answered it, not surprised to see Alexa outside. She smiled.

"Go for a walk or something?" she asked.

"Sure," Decker said. He grabbed one of the cookies Beck left and closed the door behind him as he joined her outside.

"It's a nice morning," Alexa said.

Decker glanced around. He touched his head, wincing at the spiritual assault of the people in the Square. Amber had decided to hold her class outside today. He glanced over those seated on the picnic tables. His gaze settled on Summer. As if feeling his stare, she looked over.

She smiled.

Decker looked away. Even meeting her gaze stirred his magick. He focused instead on Alexa.

"I know a good spot," Alexa said. "Wanna go?"

"Yeah."

She talked about her car and family. He tried to tune in but couldn't find the interest. Instead, he focused on the forest. Alexa walked down the road, over the wooden bridge and onward, past a secondary picnic area. They moved into the forest, to a small meadow filled with daisies. In the center was a large, flat stone. Alexa sat on it and patted the place beside her.

"Isn't this cute?" she asked.

"Yeah."

"You bring condoms?"

"What?"

"I have some."

Decker leaned away as she fished them out of her pocket. He stared at her.

"No one asks me out just to talk," she explained. "And you'd be an awesome feather in my cap. I mean, me and the Master of Night and Fire? I'll be bragging about this for the rest of my life."

"Thanks, but I really … that's not why I agreed to hang out."

"Really?"

He nodded.

"It would be cool, though," she said hopefully. "I mean, you're about to become our leader of sorts."

"Maybe," he said, unable to shake his surprise someone would want to sleep with him just because he was about to take on such an awful role. "I thought it'd be nice to hang out."

It was Alexa's turn to look surprised. She tucked the condoms back in her pocket. They were quiet for a moment, an awkward silence that reminded him he had no real interest in the girl beside him.

"So you run?" he asked at last.

"All state cross-country, all four years of high school," she replied.

"That's cool."

The silence fell again. Decker rose, looking around. Alexa stood as well and took his arm, pulling him to face her. He felt nothing at her touch, nothing like when he touched Summer. Alexa moved closer and reached up, cupping his cheeks as she kissed him. Decker mechanically returned her kisses. Desire rose in his body uncontrolled, and Alexa's hands dropped to his chest then to the zipper on his jeans.

"Not so bad, huh?" she whispered against his lips. "Trust me. You'll enjoy this as much as I will."

Decker said nothing. He forced the thought of Summer from his thoughts. He'd never deserve a girl like her, no matter what their connection was. Meaningless relations with virtual strangers would soothe his blood as much as Summer could. Alexa dropped to her knees before him, and his head dropped back with a moan.

Chapter Six

SUMMER'S FIRST WEEK passed quietly. Dance class in the morning was followed by one other class: history, personal magick with Amber, literature, or math. She'd seen Decker with a tall brunette when they had classes outside. He'd acknowledged her the first day and then, no more. The afternoons were free, and Summer managed to hide away in her room. She fed her fawn as much as she could and changed its bandage daily. It slept most of the time and lay listlessly when it wasn't sleeping.

She'd determined the animal wasn't going to make it during dance class on her tenth day there. The odd strategy used to teach them to understand their body became a soothing hour daily, and she found it was the only thing she really looked forward to. It was the only thing she was better at than any of the other girls.

After dance class on the tenth day, she returned to her room to find two surprises. The first was a note slid under the door. Summer opened it curiously.

Dear Summer, at the end of the summer, we have a dance at the resort near the beach. I wondered if you'd go with me as my date? Just leave this note under your door if so. Yours truly, Beck

Her heart leapt then almost stopped. She sat on her bed, stunned by the idea Beck secretly liked her more than a friend. With his turquoise eyes and perfect features, he could've asked any girl there, even Dawn.

But he hadn't. He'd asked *her*.

She hastily folded it again and pushed it under the door. She wanted to wait until he came to get it, then yank the door open and thank him. Guessing this would appear more desperate than grateful, she paced in front of her door, listening for anyone who came by. She heard nothing, and her eyes went to the bed.

Her deer was gone. Excitement turned to panic. She searched her room, even under the beds, before glancing towards the closet. She'd left it open and the door to her room closed. Dread in her stomach, she opened the door.

The deer was awake and alert, its legs curled beneath it as it sat in the closet. It struggled to its feet at the sight of her and ventured out of the closet carefully, its tail flickering. Summer stepped back, awed by the small animal. Its every step was graceful, its beautiful face taking in the world outside the closet with curiosity. It walked up to the dresser and stared upward, as if knowing that's where its milk was.

Summer let out a delighted laugh, thrilled for the second time that morning. She pulled the glass of milk and turkey baster off the top of the dresser and sat cross-legged with her friend. It nudged the baster. She filled it with milk and watched as the fawn sucked the milk free. Summer fed him the contents of the glass and set it down, admiring the animal. It still limped, but it looked healthier than when she found it.

After eating, it curled up on the floor near her and closed its eyes. Summer hefted it onto the bed, back into its pillow fortress. The babe looked as if it wanted to crawl free but changed its mind and settled.

She wanted to tell someone, anyone, that she'd helped the creature. The only person who knew was Decker.

Decker, who was evil, even if he had lain under the stars with her a few days ago. He didn't feel what she did when their bodies touched, or he wouldn't have walked off and avoided her the rest of the week. She'd heard the Dark girls whisper at the breakfast table that he was sleeping with a girl named Alexa.

Summer's mood dampened, until she recalled the note from Beck. She opened the door and saw it was gone. Her heart flipped in her chest.

She'd never been on a date before. She'd never been to a dance. Coming here was the best thing that ever happened to her! If the deer wasn't already sleeping, she'd squeal the way the girls had at the beach.

Another thought struck her, one that made her glee turn into fear. She'd never been to a dance with a boy. She didn't know how. Summer checked her deer one last time then closed the door behind her as she descended to the main floor. She hurried down the hall to find the dance instructor, Jessie, still in the studio.

"Excuse me, Jessie," she said as she opened the door.

Jessie looked up from her spot seated on the floor, flipping through CDs.

"Watsup, Summer?"

"Nothing. I just thought … um, I'm going to the dance at the end of the month."

"Great! Those are always a blast."

"Yeah. I don't really know how to dance with a partner, though. I was wondering if you could show me."

"Sure. Where's your partner?"

"Well …" Summer hesitated. "I don't want him to know I can't dance."

Jessie smiled. "You need someone to dance with you. Wait here."

Summer almost objected as she crossed to the door into the hallway and threw it open. Jessie looked both directions before padding towards the living area. Summer waited nervously, hoping Beck wasn't the first person she saw to ask. Maybe Adam, who had been shy but kind to her at the beach.

She heard Jessie talking to someone in the hallway and crossed her arms, praying it wasn't Beck. When Jessie appeared with Decker behind her, Summer almost gasped.

"I don't know how to dance," Decker complained.

"You'll learn together. We'll start with something simple." Jessie crossed to her iPhone, which was plugged into speakers.

Summer stared at Decker. He wore black jeans and a soft black T-shirt similar to the ones he'd given her, only it was snug on him, showing his lean frame. His dark hair was tousled, as if Jessie had caught him just as he walked in from outside. He met her gaze.

"How's … you know?" he asked.

"Good," Summer said, unable to help her smile. "He's really good. His leg is almost all better."

"That's good."

An awkward silence fell between them. Orchestral music filled the room.

"How about a waltz?" Jessie called cheerfully. "Summer, hold you your right hand out like so and Decker like this." She took their hands and placed them together.

The familiar magick trickled Summer as they touched.

"Step closer. You guys don't have the plague," Jessie said and pushed them closer together.

Summer stared at Decker's chest. He didn't have the plague, but he was evil. Amber had said so. Jessie placed his hand on her hip, and more of his magick tingled through her. Caught between panic and the surge of excitement within her, Summer didn't know what to do.

"This is simple. Decker, you lead. When he steps forward, Summer you step back."

They stumbled through the first few steps, with Decker mumbling apologies as he stepped on her toes. Summer's body felt like it was on fire. Her breathing sounded too loud in her ears.

"Step *back*, Summer," Jessie said again. "Let Decker lead!"

Decker smashed her toes, and she stumbled. He caught her as she crashed into him.

"Careful, Decker!" Jessie called.

Summer looked up, instantly caught in Decker's gaze. His grip stayed around her, pressing their bodies together. As if something clicked, she sensed his next move before he made it. She stepped back with her right foot as he stepped forward with his left. They made it through another step, then another. Their moves grew faster as they began keeping up with the music.

"Excellent!" Jessie exclaimed. "Now you've found the rhythm. *One,* two, three. *One,* two, three."

Summer couldn't look away from him. Their bodies moved as if they belonged together. Decker's warmth and magick made her feel like her insides were shaking. Jessie's voice broke through Summer's trance.

"Sorry, guys, but I can't find any of my other music. I'll download some for tomorrow. You want to come back in the morning, after your class, Summer?"

Summer broke eye contact with Decker. Immediately, they fell out of sync and stumbled. He released her and stepped away.

"Sure," she managed.

"You, too, Decker. You guys are naturals together."

Summer flushed and turned away, avoiding Decker's gaze. She'd felt it, too, the instant connection that went too deep to be normal.

"Thanks, Jessie," Summer said and hurried out of the room. She ran once she entered the hallway and sprinted up the stairs to her room.

Her hands shook. Her heart felt like it was doing cartwheels in her chest. She'd never felt this way for any guy, even Beck.

Decker was off limits. He was aligned to the Dark. She wouldn't—*couldn't*—be falling for him! Yet their connection was unlike anything she'd ever felt. In his arms, she hadn't been alone.

The deer walked up to her, and she smiled. It nudged her hand. Summer retrieved the milk and fed it. Content, the deer roamed around her room, kicking up its hind legs at one point.

"Soon, I'll have to set you free," she told it. "You're almost healthy enough."

At the thought of losing her friend, she saddened. This place caused more emotional turmoil than any other school she'd attended.

The deer continued pacing. Summer hesitated then decided to take him outside. The girls in dance class had talked about taking a hike. She went to the door and checked the hallway. It was quiet. No sounds came from the lobby, either. The deer wedged his nose in the open door. Summer bent down and lifted him, pushing the door open with her hip.

She hurried out of the house with her deer and into the forest, setting him down once they'd passed the first line of trees. He walked carefully for a few feet, sniffing the world around him. A fit of excitement made his body quiver before he leapt over a log. Summer watched, laughing, as he jumped over another then turned around and jumped to come back to her.

The forest welcomed her, the wind swirling to greet her. She pulled out the rock in her pocket and held it out, wondering if the wind would talk to her today. It played with her hair, flicking it.

The deer bounded away, this time fast. Summer waited for him to return then grew worried when he didn't. She shoved the rock in her pocket and chased after the small animal, amazed at how fast he moved. His tiny hooves barely seemed to touch the ground as he raced deep into the forest.

Summer chased him until she was breathless. At last, he slowed and stopped, tail flickering. He'd paused at the base of a massive tree that was wider than a car. Roots rose to her waist, and a hollow in the tree's base was tall enough for someone Decker's height to enter without stooping.

"Come … come here, little guy," she gasped, dropping onto a root to catch her breath.

The deer stayed where it was. It nibbled on the leaves of a huckleberry bush. He seemed to be done running, so she wiped her forehead and looked around.

He was there, the ape-man from the driveway. Summer leapt to her feet, stumbled, and fell on her backside. It raised his hands in a sign that it wouldn't hurt her.

Can you hear me?

The words came from inside her head.

Summer stared.

Nod if so.

She nodded, wondering if she'd finally gone off the deep end. Maybe all the talk about magick was a hallucination, and she was asleep in her bunk at the orphanage.

The creature sat on a tree stump near her.

I am Sam. You are new here?

Sam was ugly. Her first rational thought was that his auburn hair was a perfect shade, if it didn't cover almost every inch of his body. His eyes were like a man's, his nose and jaw like an ape's. His arms and legs were lanky, his frame over seven feet tall. He smelled like sweat and the forest, of pines and summer sun. The deer was comfortable with him, settling at his feet to sleep.

"Yes," she said at last. "I'm new."

You come to my forest often. You rescue my children. He motioned to the dozing deer.

"He needed help. What are you?"

Yeti, sasquatch, bigfoot. Your kind has many names for me. Among those that live in Priest Lake, I'm known simply as Sam.

83

"And you have … magick?"

We are balancers. We monitor good and evil. We were left here to do so, though our numbers are the smallest they've ever been.

"And your name is Sam?" she asked doubtfully.

Its chuckle was out loud, a mix between a guffaw and a cough.

"You followed me from when I was dropped off," she said. "Why?"

Curious. You have a primary and secondary magick like ours. Where you are air and earth, we are earth and air. You are strong. We sensed you arrive, believe you will change the balance.

"Change the balance. That sounds bad," she said, frowning.

Not bad. Just nature. The balance sways. It must always change, and it's been stagnant for many years now. There is good and there is evil. Sometimes, there must be a bridge between them, because they forget how much they need one another to keep the balance.

"That doesn't make much sense, when they all live in the same town."

It will. We Sams have a prophecy. We have watched and waited for thousands of years. We think you are the one we've sought.

"Great. Do I end up getting sacrificed on some altar?"

No, human. It laughed again. *You restore what has been lost.*

"The bridge."

Yes. As long as you do not turn Dark.

Her eyes went to the deer. She rose and sat on the tree root again.

"I'm not special. I'm a screw-up," she whispered. "I've failed at everything I've ever done, and I've been kicked out of every school and home I went to. I can't restore anything."

You can. The magick is within you.

"People keep saying that! It's nothing but a curse. It doesn't talk to me or guide me or help me do anything!" she said with more emotion than she wanted. "I can't make it do anything except screw up my life!"

You saved this one.

Her eyes went to her fawn. "I didn't do anything but feed him."

He would've died, if you didn't have the magick of the earth in you. Your magick is there. You just have to talk to it.

Summer sighed.

Can you not feel it?

"No."

Not in the wind or when you touch another witchling?

For a moment, she wondered if he'd seen her dancing with Decker. Her face warmed at the thought, and she ducked her head.

"Maybe," she admitted. "I feel it in the wind sometimes. And sometimes, when someone here with magick touches me I feel … alive."

You see? It's inside you. It wants to help you. If you deny it, it'll continue to mess up your life. It must be set free.

"How?"

When it calls, stop fighting it. If the wind makes you feel it, spend more time with the wind. Learn what is inside you and how to reach it.

"You sound like my dance instructor. She makes us try to stretch and use every muscle in our body, so we can get in tune with them or whatever."

85

Dance is a good way to do it. Meditation. Every human accesses his magick differently. Learn to look inward and feel what is inside you. Then, you can let it out.

"Do I really want to do that, though? I mean, it's caused me nothing but pain."

Think of it as a creature with its own mind. If you lock it away in a cage and refuse to feed or free it, it will lash out at you. You wouldn't put my child in a cage like that? Sam motioned to the deer.

"No, never."

You must not do that to yourself. Instead of closing yourself off, you must open up the part of you that makes you special.

"I've never been somewhere where that was allowed."

You are here now.

She was quiet, grappling with his words. Freeing the magick within her still sounded like a bad idea, even if she knew how to do it. She wasn't sure what to say to the hairy creature that lived in the forest.

"What else does this prophecy say? Does it say how I learn to use my magick?"

No. Only that you do.

"No one here has a how-to manual on anything," she complained.

You should go now. You will have a long walk back, and this one needs more rest before he is ready to return to my forest.

She glanced up at the sky, surprised to see the sun straight overhead. It was past noon. She recalled Decker's warning about being in the forest after dark. With her luck, she'd take hours to find her way home.

"Okay, I guess. Thank you, Sam."

When she looked down from the sky, he was gone. Summer twisted to survey the area around her, surprised. She knelt and picked up the deer, setting it on its feet.

"Sam, can you tell me which way to go?" she asked into the air.

The bigfoot didn't return, didn't answer.

Summer pulled the rocks Amber gave her from her pocket. She held them up and closed her eyes, trying to figure out where inside her the magick was. She didn't feel anything, except hungry from missing lunch.

"Please take me home," she said.

The magick within her stirred as it usually did before the world around her came crashing down. Her grip tightened around the rocks, and she held her breath, terrified of what might happen this time. The tickle grew in her body until it spread from her toes to the top of her scalp. It was nothing like she felt when Decker touched her that morning, but it was there nonetheless.

Suddenly, the wind rushed through her again, pushing her in one direction. Summer opened her eyes. She stepped in that direction. It nudged her again, and she took another step.

Fear made her stomach churn as she let her magick touch that of the wind. The wind guided her gently towards the way it wanted her to go. She didn't know where it was taking her and glanced back to make sure the deer followed her. An hour later, she emerged onto the driveway leading up to the house.

"Thank you, wind," she said awkwardly.

Adam was on the porch this afternoon, fiddling with his smartphone. Summer approached him. The deer trailed. Its head and tail drooped in exhaustion. Summer sat on the porch while the deer nibbled grass on the front lawn.

"He's real neat," Adam said. "Is he yours?"

"For now," she replied. "I rescued him after his mama was hurt. He's an orphan, like me."

"What's his name?"

She smiled. "I don't know."

"Don't call him Bambi. It's gotta be something better." Adam's gaze turned thoughtful. "How about Doug?"

"Really?" she asked, nose wrinkling. "That's not a good name for a deer."

"Tarzan!"

Summer laughed.

"Definitely Tarzan," Adam said. "Just because he doesn't live in a jungle or swing from trees doesn't mean he can't be Tarzan."

"Okay, I like Tarzan."

"Did you find out what your magick is? I'm water. Which is weird, because I don't like being in water."

"Air."

"So, like, can you make storms?" he asked.

"I have no idea. I don't think my magick likes me," she said. Her thoughts went to the discussion with Sam about how she'd kept her magick caged and starved her whole life. She'd treated it the way the orphanage treated her. "Have you learned how to um, you know, tap into your magick here?"

"Yes. It's a slow process. I think, for me, the hardest part was just figuring out that it's okay to have magick. It isn't anywhere else."

"I know that feeling. That's what scares me about leaving here."

"It's not bad. Once you learn to control it, you can leave here without anyone knowing. I had no control. Whenever I had bad dreams, I'd flood our family's bean fields," Adam said. "It was okay during a drought, but during the rainy season, I ruined our crops."

"Oh, that's rough."

He shrugged. "Happens, I guess. We all ended up here because we're special. I think we all have these kinds of dark stories."

Summer leaned her head against the pole behind her. Adam's gaze returned to his smartphone, and he was quiet.

"Did you have to choose if you're on the good or evil path yet?" she voiced quietly.

"On my seventeenth birthday. All of us do on our seventeenth."

"Why seventeenth?"

"Amber says it's some ancient rite of passage." He shrugged again. "Old enough to decide, not too old to keep learning about our gifts."

"I'll be seventeen in less than a month," she said. "A couple of weeks after the dance."

"Hey, um, speaking of the dance. I was wondering if ..." He trailed off, his face growing red. "Um, do you want to go with me? Not as a date, if you don't want. We can go as friends."

"Someone else asked me. But if I can learn to dance by then, I'll dance with you," she offered. Adam was sweet and kind. She didn't want to drive him off.

"That's cool." The flush across his face grew redder, and he focused hard on the screen of his smartphone. "If you ever want to go get ice cream again, I can show you some water tricks."

"I'd like that," she replied. "I don't like to be in water, either."

"We can hang out on the beach."

"Um, Adam, have you met Sam?"

"Sam? No. Another new person?"

"Never mind. I probably got the name wrong," she murmured. Sam had openly sought her out. He'd said she was special, but she couldn't imagine being the only person Sam spoke to.

"Hey, guys," Dawn said, pushing open the screen door. "You're such a cute couple! Out here on the porch talking!"

Adam ignored her, gaze on his phone.

"You'll have to come to the beach next time, Adam. We're both water elements! We can have some fun."

When he made no effort to look at her, Dawn's attention turned to Summer.

"Where have you been? You always disappear after our morning sessions." The blond girl sat down beside Summer, bringing with her a cloud of flowery perfume.

"In my room," Summer replied. "Reading and stuff."

"You have to come out with us. Tonight is movie night. Did Adam invite you?"

"I'm not going," Adam said.

"You should come anyway," Dawn continued. "We rarely get to leave after dark. Amber is taking us all to the mall, so even if you don't like movies, we can hang out."

"No." Adam's response was blunt.

"Um, I'll think about it," Summer said.

"Oh, I insist. You have to come!" Dawn said. She rose. "We'll leave in a couple of hours. I can help you pick out some clothes for the dance or something."

"I really—"

"See you later!"

When the blond girl had left, Adam set his phone down.

"You can just tell her no," he said. "She's a psycho."

90

"She doesn't seem that bad," Summer replied. "I can't afford clothes anyway. I didn't even think about what to wear to the dance."

"You want me to lend you some money?" He reached into his pocket and pulled out his wallet.

"No."

"You can't go to the mall and let the psycho show you up." He pulled out two twenty-dollar bills. "How much do dresses cost anyway?"

Summer shrugged. "We only had handouts at the orphanage. I don't want your money, Adam. I don't know how I'd pay you back."

"Show her up at the dance. That's all I ask."

Summer's gaze lingered on the money. She did want to look nice for Beck, and she had less than twenty dollars she'd saved from the travel money the orphanage gave her.

She took his money. He smiled.

"My parents are well off," he said. "They don't care what I spend."

"Must be nice."

"Sometimes. And sometimes, it's a pain, because people always want money or something from you."

"Is that why Dawn's so nice to you when you're not nice to her?"

"Yeah." He grinned.

"I'll do my best. She's like, perfect, though, so I doubt I can look half as good as she does," Summer said.

"She's nice to you because all the guys here talk about you. You're prettier and nicer. Even Beck says so."

"You guys talk about me?"

"Guys gossip, too," he said. "We just talk about girls instead of shoes or whatever girls talk about."

Beck thought she was pretty. She had to suppress her smile. She thought of Decker and couldn't help wondering if he thought the same. Would she feel with Beck what she felt with Decker when they went to the dance?

"I've never been called pretty before," she said. "This place is so weird. I keep waiting for the dream to be over and to wake up in the orphanage again."

"It's real. It's not all good, but it's better here than anywhere else for people like us, especially after your seventeenth birthday."

"I hope you're right. I never want to go back to LA. I think I could live here my whole life," she said.

"Really? You don't miss stores and civilization?"

"No. I want to stay with the forest."

"A lot of those with magick stay here. The Turner twins have a cabin on the other side of the lake. Their family comes here to ski in winter and sometimes in summer. I think their parents have magick talents, too."

"I didn't know they were so rich."

"Their dad owns a lot of real estate in New York City. They have houses all over the world."

"Wow."

She couldn't help thinking Beck would want nothing to do with a poor orphan like her. The idea upset her. She looked towards her deer, which was nibbling at one of the bushes against the house.

"I'm going inside," she said and rose. Tarzan followed her up the stairs and into the house. Summer hurried through the house, hoping no one caught them. They made it to her room, and she saw two more notes on the floor.

The fawn leapt onto her bed and curled up in the middle. Summer sat on the edge, overwhelmed by her meeting with Sam. She'd felt her magick for a moment in the forest, and it led her home. Now, she didn't feel it.

Her attention went to the notes. She opened the first, recognizing the handwriting.

Dearest Summer, I was thinking about you today. Your skin is so pretty, and I love your smile. I can't wait to dance with you. But please don't tell anyone we're going together. I'm breaking up with Dawn that night. She goes crazy sometimes, and I don't want her to ruin our first dance. Love, Beck

She frowned, thinking of Dawn. While the girl embarrassed her a lot, Summer still felt bad for her. The second note was all compliments on her hair and smile, and she read it twice, feeling as if she was floating.

A knock on the door preceded Amber's entrance. Summer sprang up, surprised. Amber's clear gaze went from her to the deer.

"I can explain," Summer said quickly. "Please don't send me away!"

Amber smiled and closed the door. She sat on the other bed. The deer watched her.

"He was hurt, and his mother was dead, so I rescued him. I won't keep him, because I know the rule about pets, but I just wanted to make sure he was okay before he went back to the forest. Please, *please* don't send me back to the orphanage!" Summer's head began to hurt as fear filled her.

"I won't send you back," Amber said. "Really, it's okay, Summer. I understand. Your elements will make you more sensitive to the forest and its creatures."

"You're not mad?"

"I can't be mad when you're following your nature. What's his name?"

"Tarzan."

Amber laughed. "How long have you had him?"

"A little over a week. I found him in the forest one night when I got lost trying to get back to the house. His mama was killed, and his leg was hurt. Decker ..." Summer trailed off, recalling his dark eyes and magickal touch.

"Found you?"

"Yeah. He helped me bring Tarzan back."

"You're lucky," Amber said, growing serious. "You shouldn't be in the forest after dark."

"Why is that? I mean, I didn't do it on purpose, and Decker warned me not to do it again."

"There are a lot of wild animals out at night. Cougars, bears, the like. And, well, those who use Dark magick are in the forest at night training. You don't want to get caught up in one of their spells. They won't purposely hurt you, but accidents happen."

The way she said the words made Summer shudder.

"Anyway, I came by to see if you're coming with us to the mall. Dawn seems convinced you are."

"I think I'll go," Summer said slowly. "I want to get something for the dance."

"Oh, good. Is Tarzan okay in here alone?"

"Yes. He'll just sleep. You're sure you're not mad?"

"No, Summer, I'm not. You're doing what your elements guide you to do. When I said no pets, I meant no dogs or cats, just because you want one. Tarzan is a different case altogether. Okay?"

Summer nodded, relieved.

"We'll leave in half an hour." Amber smiled again and left.

Summer released her breath. She got ready and went to the porch to wait. Adam was gone. A white van pulled up long before any of the other girls were ready. Finally Amber corralled them down the stairs and into the van.

Summer sat in the back, the forty dollars Adam gave her in her pocket. She'd never had forty dollars before, and she wondered if she could really buy a dress that would make Dawn drool. The girls talked the entire hour-and-a-half drive.

Summer was relieved when they got to the mall and left the confines of the van.

"Meet back here in two hours," Amber called as the girls moved away from the van.

"Summer, come on!" Dawn called over her shoulder. "Dresses!"

Summer trailed. Dawn always dressed pretty; she had to know where to find nice clothes. The girls ignored her and talked amongst themselves. Summer took in the mall and its shoppers and stores. She'd been to a mall twice in her life. This one looked smaller than the one she'd gone to in LA. She smiled as she walked, enjoying the sight of so many different colors.

Dawn led them into a store filled with chic dresses and outfits. It looked expensive, which Summer confirmed when she examined the tag of the first dress she came to.

"Two hundred dollars." Her mouth almost dropped open. She looked around her, marveling at the dresses but knowing there was nothing there she could afford.

"Summer, what size are you?" Dawn asked. "I'll pull some dresses I think you'll look good in."

"No, I think—"

"Come on!" Dawn said with a roll of her eyes. She disappeared behind a rack of dresses. "Size four? I know you're not a size zero like me."

Summer's face warmed. She didn't know what size she was. Her clothes were in all sizes and some were men's. Dawn didn't wait for her answer but roamed the store, selecting a few dresses. Summer trailed, arms crossed. She couldn't afford anything here.

"Take these and try them on," Dawn directed. She piled four dresses into Summer's arms.

Summer almost refused then caved, admiring the materials and colors. She had to look good for Beck, or he'd regret asking her to the dance. She took the dresses into a dressing room and changed into the first one slowly.

Dawn was right about her size. Summer zipped the first one and took a deep breath before facing the mirror. When she did, her breath caught. The form-fitting dress was soft against her skin—and fit better than any piece of clothing she owned. She'd never noticed her curves or how womanly they'd become. She still felt like the awkward eleven-year-old with boobs too big for her skinny frame.

The mirror painted a different story. Her dark hair framed a face with delicate features and large, brown eyes. Her skin was tanned from the California summer sun, and the cut of the dress made her legs look long on her otherwise short frame. She had hips now. They were round and balanced out her breasts.

"Summer, come on!" Dawn said, knocking on the door. "Show us!"

Summer did, suspecting Dawn wouldn't take no for an answer. She opened the door to the dressing room and stepped out. It took all her willpower not to cross her arms. The three girls with Dawn smiled. Dawn looked agitated.

"Perfect!" one of them said.

"It's okay," Dawn said. "That color's not good on you."

Summer looked down. She liked the blue-green color of the dress. It matched Beck's eyes.

"Try on the next one," Dawn ordered.

Summer returned to the dressing room. The next one was silver. When she stepped out, Dawn was there as well, twirling in a skin-tight red dress.

"You have to get this one, Dawn," one of the other girls gushed. "You'll knock him off his feet!"

"Hmm, I'm not sure," Dawn said.

"You look beautiful," Summer seconded, taking in the leggy blond's perfect, slender body. She felt guilty again about the note Beck had given her. Dawn didn't know what was in store for her at the dance.

"Oh, thanks. You look good, too," Dawn said with an insincere smile.

Summer looked in the mirror. Behind Dawn, she looked like a short, fat star. She returned to the dressing room, not wanting to try on any more.

"Try the blue one, Summer!" Dawn called. "You need to get a new bra, too. That one looks like you've owned it for years."

I have, Summer said to herself, looking at the ratty, off-white bra in the mirror. Embarrassed, she tucked the straps down when she tried on the blue one. One look in the mirror, and she fell in love with the A-line style that hugged her curves and ended above her knees. Of all the dresses, it was the plainest, with a scoop neck and cap sleeves.

"That's it!" one of the other girls exclaimed as she stepped out.

"Definitely," another echoed. "Dawn, you have to see her!"

Dawn emerged in another tight number, this one gold sequins. Summer turned to face her. Dawn's gaze swept over her, unimpressed.

"Yeah, that's the best one of them," she agreed. "I don't think you'll find anything that'll fit you better, until you lose some of that weight."

Summer's face grew hot. She'd never looked as beautiful as she did in the dress. Dawn pulled the tag free.

"It's on sale, too," she said. "One fifty. I say you get it."

"Um, I'm not sure," Summer said.

"Look at yourself," Dawn said and pushed her to the mirror. "What will your date think when he sees you?"

Summer smiled.

"You're a doll," Dawn said. "You have to buy it."

"I really can't," Summer replied. "I think I'll just keep looking."

"You won't find anything better," Dawn said. "This complements your skin tone and eyes and everything else."

Summer stared at herself, growing more dismayed the longer she wore the dress. She could never afford it. Or any dress, if they were all so expensive.

"Think about it," Dawn said and went back to her dressing room.

Summer returned to hers. She looked at the remaining dress on the hanger then peeked out of the dressing room. The other girls had returned to their rooms, too, to change into the next dress. She looked at her ill-fitting clothes then at the dresses.

She shouldn't have succumbed to Dawn's encouragement. She should've gone to the department store and looked for a sale. She put her clothes back on.

"Dawn, this is a little out of my price range," she said. "I'm going to keep looking. I'll see you guys later."

"There's a Goodwill here," Dawn called innocently. "Maybe you can afford something there."

The other girls laughed, and Dawn joined them. Summer left the store, face hot. She'd been to a Goodwill before. Even if Dawn ridiculed it, Summer had found some good finds there. She shook off the sense of humiliation that had plagued her at every school she went to. She was going to the dance with Beck, the most handsome boy in the world. Suddenly, she didn't feel quite so guilty about Dawn getting dumped at the dance.

Summer sneaked a look over her shoulder to make sure Dawn didn't follow her to ridicule her more. She entered the Goodwill store and began to browse. Goodwill had nothing like the nice store Dawn took her to.

Just when Summer gave up, she saw a shimmer of pale, metallic pink. She dug through the rack and pulled out the dress, a rather plain prom dress, by the looks of it. Checking the tag, she was happy to find it was a 4-6, around her size. She examined it for any stains she'd have to get out at home. It needed to be washed, but it was pretty. The price read twenty-five dollars.

Thrilled with her find, she slung it over her arm and went to the section with ladies underwear. Dawn's comment about her bra hit home. Summer tried on a few before finding one that fit.

She left the store with her purchases, pleased with the treasures she'd found. She had enough money for the food court and walked by the different restaurants, awed by the ability to choose what she ate for the first time since she was a child. She went with pizza, milkshake, and cake.

Full and content, Summer went back to the place where Amber had dropped them off. It was past dark, and the mall parking lot was full. She sat and waited. The air grew chilly, and she sat at the base of the fountain, huddling to keep her body warm.

She waited and waited. Cars began to leave the lot, and the night grew darker. Summer got up and paced to keep warm and look for the van or girls. She saw neither and sat down to wait again.

When the last car pulled out of the parking lot, she knew they'd forgotten her. She hugged her knees to her chest. She would have expected others to leave her, but not Amber. Shivering from the cold, Summer stayed where she was.

When the moon was directly overhead, the white van pulled into the parking lot. Summer uncurled and stood. Amber threw open the door.

"I am so sorry, Summer!" she exclaimed and threw her arms around her. "You're so cold!"

Summer said nothing as Amber ushered her into the van.

"You can lay down on one of the seats. Here's a blanket. I can't believe … this is going too far," Amber muttered.

"I'm sorry. I didn't mean to," Summer said, frowning.

"Not you, honey. Just get some sleep on the way back."

Summer studied her. Amber was upset for the first time since Summer had met her. She said nothing, though, and Summer blamed herself. She wrapped the blanket around her before stretching out on a bench seat. Exhausted and warm, she managed to fall asleep soon after they left the parking lot.

Chapter Seven

THE NEXT MORNING, Summer ate a fast breakfast, tardy to start her day after getting home so late. She drank her juice as she hurried down the hallway to the dance studio. Jessie had already started, and Summer slid into the back of class. She was tired and went through the morning routine without paying much attention. As she turned to leave, Jessie stopped her.

"Don't rush off, Summer!"

Summer moved out of the way of the other girls. Dawn caught her gaze and smiled. Summer smiled back. When they'd left, she approached Jessie.

"Did you forget?" Jessie asked.

"Forget what?"

"Your dance lesson."

"Oh." Summer kicked herself mentally. "I'm kind of tired today, Jessie. Maybe we can—"

"Right on time, Decker," Jessie said, glancing towards the door.

Summer turned to face him, at once caught in his dark gaze. From the distance, she felt his magick. It energized her even without touching him.

"Sorry to interrupt. What was that, Summer?" Jessie asked.

"Nothing," Summer murmured.

"Waltz to warm up and we'll move onto something else," Jessie told them.

Summer moved to the middle of the floor. Decker joined her. He reached for her then rubbed the back of his head nervously. Her own body was warm and tingly before she lifted her hand out. He placed his against it then stepped forward with more confidence and placed his other hand on the small of her back.

Her senses came alive again. She recalled what Sam had said, that she needed to find what made her magick sing. It was Decker.

"Have you ever ... met Sam?" she asked, gazing up at him as they danced.

"Yes. Only a few of us have spoken to him. You met him?"

"Yesterday."

"You must be of certain interest to his kind. They don't talk to just anyone."

She said nothing. Instead, she listened to her body, the way Sam said she should. It responded to Decker, whose lead turned from hesitant to firm. Her lightheadedness returned, and she hoped he couldn't tell just how hard her heart was beating.

"You look tired," he said. "Did your deer keep you up?"

"No," she said. "I went to the mall yesterday and got left behind."

"Amber left you?"

"Just an accident. I'm too quiet. I guess I'm easy to forget."

"I don't think so."

Her face grew hot, and she looked away.

"Today, a merengue and salsa!" Jessie said. "I feel like something more fast-paced. This way, when you're listening to that modern crap, you can go between the slow and the quick. Summer, stand on my right. Decker, on my left. We'll work on the salsa steps first."

Summer stepped away from Decker. Jessie pulled her to the side as Latin music blared into the studio. Summer stumbled through the fast-paced steps that seemed only to tangle her feet. She couldn't keep up with the music, even when she mastered the steps. Frustrated, she sneaked a glance at Decker. He was worse off, his large feet tripping him as he tried to dance. They struggled through it for half an hour, with Jessie barking commands at them.

"On your toes, Decker. I know you played football," Jessie said impatiently. "You both are so much more coordinated at this when ..."

Summer gave up with a sigh. Jessie was gazing at her intently.

"Try it together," the instructor said.

Summer looked at Decker, who held out his hand. She took it.

"Okay, one, two, three," Decker said quietly.

They stepped together. Again and again, easily keeping pace with the music and each other. Her body flowed with the rhythm.

Jessie turned off the music. "I don't think you guys need lessons. Just go to the dance together."

Summer kept quiet, uncertain if Decker knew who her date was.

"I don't go to the dances," Decker said. "So you might as well keep teaching us."

"You sassin' me?" Jessie asked with a grin.

"No, Jessie. Summer's transition hasn't been easy. You might as well help her adjust."

Summer stared at him, surprised he'd talk that way to an instructor.

Decker didn't know what got into him, but he was angry at Jessie. Summer's body was relaxed in his arms, fitting against his in a way that seemed too natural. Her breasts were pressed against his chest. He'd thought the first day of dancing was torture, but today, the sensations were worse. Her magick didn't just call to him, it compelled him to her, like a paperclip to a magnet. It made his whole body ache in a way he'd never experienced.

He wanted her. Bad, and in more ways than he could identify. The rise and fall of her chest, the way she looked up at him ... the desire he felt with Alexa was purely physical. He knew now this was something else, something primal.

"Alright, we'll keep dancing," Jessie said. She put on music then stood back to watch.

"Thank you, I think," Summer said, looking up at Decker.

"Sorry. I want to do this right for you," he said.

The connection between them grew stronger. He took in her brown eyes and long eyelashes, the pink flush across her face, the way she yielded to him when he held her. He'd hoped Alexa and keeping his distance would quell their connection, but it only grew stronger. They didn't even need to talk; magick moved between their bodies. As if they were one, not two individuals.

It was impossible to deny there was more between them than he could figure out. He'd debated not coming, but disappointing Summer had seemed worse than the torture of dancing with her.

"I have a favorite constellation," he said. "Scorpio."

"Beautiful constellation, tragic story," she murmured. "You know in mythology, Scorpio killed Orion, right?"

"Uh, no, I didn't." His face grew red. Was this a sign he should walk away from her for good? "Why are you so interested in stars?"

"I guess I'm not really. I had nothing to do at the orphanage, especially between schools. I used to read a lot. One of the other kids left textbooks out, so I read through the astronomy one and started trying to find the stars," she replied. "I read a lot of Shakespeare and other literature."

"I've read some Shakespeare. It's a little over my head," he admitted.

"I think there's beauty in his work. And tragedy. Always tragedy." Her voice grew soft, sad.

"Sorta like life."

"Yeah. Though being here, I've learned there's hope, too."

Jessie's phone rang.

Decker clamped his mouth shut. He wanted to say hope was for naïve fools, but he couldn't. Summer's eyes glowed with a light that hadn't been there when she arrived, and her soul no longer sang its lonesome song. She'd found hope in the place where he lost his.

"I meant to tell you yesterday, thank you for dancing with me," she said. "Even though you don't go to dances and even though you probably have something better to do."

"It's my pleasure, Summer. Really."

"Come back tomorrow morning," Jessie said. "I'll have more music. Decker, Matty wants to see you."

Decker rolled his eyes. Summer smiled, broke contact, and turned away. He watched her leave, agitation filling him. Her touch silenced the noise in his head and soothed him in a way nothing else could.

"Thanks, Jessie," he said and left the studio.

Matilda, the head instructor for the Dark arts, had an office in the small attachment to the garage, opposite Amber's. Decker went to her office and knocked, waiting for her to beckon him to open it before entering. Tall and svelte, Matilda wore her hair short and was almost always in a suit or business clothing. She wore a white blouse and pencil skirt today.

"Have a seat, Decker." Her voice held a slight rasp that took the edge off her severe façade.

He sat in front of her. She pushed her laptop away and leaned back, focusing on him.

"How you holding up?" she asked.

"Good enough."

"Your parents are concerned, and so are your teachers."

"Not sure what they expect. It's not like I'm getting a new job at the mall or something," he snapped.

"I understand that. I think your adjustment period will be brutal. I was here when your mother took her place. It nearly killed her to lose her sister and face the Dark alone. If not for your father, she wouldn't have made it."

106

"They won't even be here for my birthday, so there's no help for me," he said.

"The kids say you're dating Alexa. Any sort of connection there, like your parents have?"

"It's physical, nothing more."

Matilda shook her head. "Damn teens and hormones. At least you own up to it. Amber doesn't believe me when I tell her half the kids here are sexually active."

"More than half," Decker said, smiling.

"I'm not surprised. But on a serious note, Decker" — Matilda leaned forward— "you're in danger of going over the edge if you've got no one here to support you. Maybe your mother doesn't remember what she went through during the transition. It wasn't pretty."

"I'll be fine."

"I'm telling you, you won't."

"What do you want me to do about it?" Decker ran his fingers through his hair with a frustrated sigh. He suspected as much. Whatever happened to him on his eighteenth birthday, he'd turn into a soul-stealing assassin.

"Are you and Beck getting along better?"

"Yeah."

"Maybe that'll do. I'd hoped Alexa was the Michael Turner to your Rania," Matilda said. "Are you sure she's not?"

"Why does it matter?" he demanded.

"There's only been one Master of Fire and Night who didn't have a partner when he assumed his powers. The Deathbringer, Bartholomew the Terrible. I don't know for sure if this is why he went insane, but it's a pattern I won't ignore."

He met her gaze, well aware of the horror stories of the Dark Master who'd not only gone insane, but spent his tenure annihilating Light witchlings, Dark witchlings and humans alike. He'd reigned longest of all the Masters, simply because none of the women he raped survived long enough to bear a child. One finally did and birthed twins who worked together to slay their mad father and reestablish the balance.

Decker stood and paced, staring out the window. Summer and the little Indian girl he thought was named Biji were walking towards one of the picnic tables. Summer was smiling. The sight soothed him physically and mentally. For a moment, he forgot about Matilda's horrific words about his potential fate. His shoulders eased, and he breathed more deeply.

He had a partner. But he'd never expose her to what he'd become.

"The new girl?" Matilda's approach was silent. "Or is it just physical attraction?"

"It's neither," he said sharply. "Leave Summer out of this."

The instructor raised an eyebrow. She stepped away and held up a hand as he turned on her.

"As you wish," she said calmly.

Unable to explain his sudden fury, Decker watched her as she returned to her seat behind the desk and folded her hands over her knee. She waited, unafraid of the shadows that leaked from his body at his emotion. Finally, he rolled his shoulders and took a deep breath.

"Please," he added, aware it was too late.

"Of course."

"Whatever happens, I'll deal with it. Alone."

Matilda said nothing more. Decker glanced towards the benches again then turned and strode out of her office and down the hall, towards the kitchen. Food and the forest were the best he could do at soothing the fire within him. The last he'd heard, Kenny's shadow demon had failed to kill the person who hurt his brother. His brother died yesterday evening.

Kenny didn't have the magick to exact his revenge, but Decker did. He'd unleash the fury within him upon the fool who killed a child. Maybe then, he'd feel some peace. He went to the kitchen for some food first.

Butterflies were in Summer's stomach when she returned to her room. She told herself they shouldn't be; she was going to the dance with Beck. Besides, Decker had a girlfriend. His magick had left her body by the time she returned to her room, where one of the girls waited for her outside her door.

"Your name is Summer, right?" The beautiful girl was around her age with large brown eyes and dark bronze skin.

"Yes."

"I'm Biji."

"I remember," Summer said.

"I heard, um, you have a deer. Can I see him?"

"Sure." Summer opened the door to her room. The small animal was curled up on the bed and raised its head.

"They said his name is Tarzan," Biji said and giggled.

"It is."

"He's beautiful." Biji leaned over to peer at the creature. Her waist-length braid fell over her shoulder onto the bed, and Tarzan nibbled on it.

"How long have you been here?" Summer asked, sitting down on the bed.

"About a year. I'm an air element. Amber said you were, too, and maybe I can teach you some things."

"That'd be awesome," Summer said, her interest in the small girl growing. "Is it hard to learn?"

"Not really. Well, once you unlock it, it's all about control. But unlocking your magick is the hardest part."

"Why?"

Biji shrugged. "Maybe because we suppress it for sixteen years and then have to figure out how to stop doing that."

"So what did you do to make your magick unlocked?"

"You'll know. You'll feel what makes it sing."

Decker. Summer didn't like the instinct that reminded her of how the tall, handsome loner made her feel.

"For me, it was bungee jumping!" Biji's face glowed. "I love it!"

"I don't think I want to try that."

"Do you want to come outside? I'll show you some of the things I can do."

Summer nodded. Biji patted Tarzan and led Summer out, down the stairs and to one of the picnic tables in the courtyard.

"Okay, sit down and watch," Biji said.

Summer sat on the table, puzzled as Biji scrambled over to the nearest pine tree and began to climb it. The small teen was nimble and coordinated, reaching the halfway point fifty feet up within a few minutes.

"Are you watching?" she called.

"Yes!" Summer replied, shielding her eyes against the sun.

Biji swan-dived out of the tree. Summer yelped, horrified. Just before Biji should've hit the ground, she stopped in midair. She was laughing. She dropped her feet to the ground and stood.

"What do you think?" she asked, beaming.

"My god!" Summer breathed. Her heart was in her ears and her pulse flying.

"We control the air," Biji said. She swirled her hand in the air. A pinecone from the ground rose and landed in her palm.

"I can float?"

"Someday, when you can use your magick." Biji tossed the pinecone. "You don't know what the trigger ... ooohh." Her last word came out as a half-sigh.

Summer followed her gaze. Decker emerged from the side door, sandwich in one hand and a soda in his other. His dark clothing did little to diminish his muscular form. If he saw them, he ignored them.

"All the girls are in love with him," Biji whispered.

"I thought they were in love with his brother," Summer said.

"Secretly, they want Decker. Even Dawn. I mean, the tall, brooding bad boy? Like from a romance novel. I wonder what he looks like with his shirt off."

Summer smiled at Biji's eager tone. "So your trigger wasn't a person?"

"He never gives any of us in the Light the time of day," Biji went on. "The Dark girls can. He's slept with a few over the year I've been here. You know it's because they have some sort of secrets about sex."

Summer laughed out of amusement and embarrassment.

"Have you ever you know ... done it?" Biji asked.

Summer shook her head.

"Me neither. I guess I'll know someday."

Summer laughed harder at Biji's disappointed look. The small girl grinned then lifted more things in the air. Summer watched, marveling. Biji formed small clouds in her hands

111

and sent them over to Summer. They rained on her feet, making her smile. When Biji was done with her tricks, she sat beside Summer on the table.

"I heard you were hanging out with Dawn. You don't really seem like the type to hang out with her," Biji said.

"I don't really," Summer said. "She doesn't seem that bad. Everyone says she is."

"Oh, she's that bad."

Summer shrugged.

"If she doesn't see you as a threat, she'll leave you alone. It might be good she's not messing with you."

"I'm nowhere near as pretty as she is, and I'm poor," Summer said. "There's nothing she can be jealous of."

"Whatever," Biji said, rolling her eyes. "It's good you don't hang out with her. Are you going to the dance?"

"Yes."

"Did someone ask you or are you just gonna hang out with me?"

"Someone asked me."

"Who?" Biji demanded. "I heard you're going out with Adam?"

"No, we're not going out," Summer said with a shake of her head. "Beck asked me."

"Beck? Really?"

"Yes. Why?"

"He's dating Dawn. At least, I thought he was." Biji looked puzzled. "But if he asked you, maybe they're over with."

"Maybe. I don't know," she said vaguely, mind on the note about Beck breaking up with Dawn. "Are you going with anyone?"

"No. No one asked. I thought about asking someone, though."

Decker emerged from one of the dorms, trailed by three other guys in black. Biji's gaze was glued to the Dark twin as they crossed to the house.

"Decker?" Summer prompted. She crossed her arms, not sure why she cared if Biji wanted to go with Decker.

"Yeah. But he never goes to them anyway."

"So you said that bungee jumping or whatever is what unlocked your power?"

"Yes! I jumped off a building," Biji replied.

"Are like, people ever the triggers to unlock magick?"

"Anything can be. But a person ... that seems like it'd be very weird. I mean, how would that work? You basically have to totally surrender to whatever it is and then, the magick unlocks."

"I'm not sure," Summer said. "It doesn't sound like someone can be the trigger."

"It's probably possible, but I don't know." Biji's gaze narrowed. "Why do you ask? You think Beck is your trigger?"

"Not Beck. I mean, no. I just wondered."

"Just wondered. Hmm."

"Really."

"Whatever. Did they show you the creek?"

"No."

Biji hopped off the table and started towards the road. Summer joined her, and they walked down the daisy-and-pine-tree lined road past the dorms and deeper into the forest. After ten minutes, they came to an old, wooden bridge leading over a creek a few feet wide. Biji stopped in the middle of the bridge and leaned over the side.

Summer did so as well. Clear water about three feet deep rushed over rocks below the bridge. She saw a few small fish and even more bright rocks in the shallows of the creek. The flow of water made a soothing sound, one that took her thoughts off of magick and Decker. Biji led her off the bridge and to a large, flat rock beside the creek. She sprawled on her back and stared at the sky.

"You ever make shapes out of clouds?" she asked.

Summer shook her head, liking the girl more and more.

"It's about all there is to do here," Biji complained. "Unless you like playing games. I don't."

"I don't know how to play many games," Summer replied. She lay down beside her. Trees and a few cottony clouds were all that marred the brilliant blue sky. "I can play poker and blackjack."

"You'll have to teach me."

Summer gazed at the clouds, content with the creek's soft gurgle and the sun's gentle warmth. The air swirled around them, and Biji swatted it away.

"Do you see anything?" Biji asked.

Summer concentrated. "An elephant? I don't know."

"I see it! He's playing basketball, right?"

Summer giggled.

"We have a lot of elephants in India. They're so big. When you see them on the telly, you can't tell how big they really are. They can crush a car with their foot."

"Do you miss India?"

"Yes and no. I miss my family but when I go back, I have to get married. So, I'd rather stay here."

"You *have* to get married?" Summer asked.

"My family arranged a marriage for me. He's a nice guy. But I just want to roam around the world."

"Wow. That's crazy. Maybe he'll travel with you."

"Maybe. Ruins my chances with Decker, though."

"How does that work?" Summer asked. "I mean, he's evil. You can't be on the side of Light and date someone who's evil."

"Yeah you can. It's like dating anyone else. The Dark is like a career choice. You wouldn't *not* date someone because he was like, a dentist or something."

"I think good and evil are a bit more serious than dating a dentist!"

"But it's really not," Biji insisted. "A lot of Light and Dark date and get married. The Turner twins' parents did that."

"That doesn't make the person on the Light side go to hell or anything?"

Biji laughed. "No! If anything, it made Beck and Decker more powerful. They each have two elements, and rumor has it that Decker has three."

"What are their elements?"

"Beck is air and earth; Decker is the rest."

"Meaning ..." Summer pushed.

"Fire, water, spirit."

"The exact opposite of me."

"Who? Decker?"

"Yeah."

"You've got a crush on him, too, don't you?" Biji exclaimed.

"No—"

"It's okay. I was beginning to think you were weird. I mean, who wouldn't?"

Summer was quiet. She didn't know what she felt when she was with the intense Dark twin. She understood the simple attraction she felt towards Beck. It was easier to focus on the Light twin.

"The summer dance is in three days. Maybe you should go with him instead of Beck. That way Dawn doesn't get jealous or go psycho on you," Biji said.

"She's been nice to me so far."

"Everyone thinks that, until she tries to stab you in the back," Biji replied. "I've seen it happen to a lot of girls here, ones not nearly as pretty as you are."

"I'm not pretty. I just have a big chest," Summer said with an awkward laugh.

"To men, that's pretty. I'm totally jealous. Do you eat anything special to get those?"

"I don't think so. I think they're hereditary."

"Ah," Biji sighed. "Then I'm screwed."

They giggled. After an hour of cloud watching, they returned to the main house for lunch and to check on Tarzan. Biji led her to their sole afternoon class, a two-hour block on math and science that left Summer close to dozing. There were Dark girls in this class, and she concentrated on them rather than the dry lecture. They all wore black, some in heavy make-up while others wore none. They seemed as diverse as the Light girls.

Biji's comparison of the Dark path to a regular career path did little to make Summer understand how being Dark could be any less evil. The girls didn't turn into monsters in class, yet they'd done something to *earn* their way to the Dark. She wondered what, and if they regretted their choices or were as content as the Light girls.

What had Decker done? Was it why he was always alone?

She didn't want to think about him, but her body remembered too well how she felt in his arms. Her magick sang only for him.

The class dismissed, jarring her out of her thoughts. Summer rose from the desk and closed her notebook. She hadn't written down anything from the course. To date, no one had mentioned tests, and she hoped it was because there were none.

She retreated to her room to clean up after Tarzan then take him outside before the mandatory dinner in an hour. Summer closed the screen door on the front porch behind her. Tarzan wandered out onto the front lawn, his limp still apparent. She caught the flash of auburn against the green curtain of pine trees down the road and stepped off the porch.

Glancing around, she made sure no one was watching her then went towards Sam. Tarzan trailed, his mouth filled with green grass. Summer pushed fragrant pine branches aside to enter the forest. She didn't see Sam and ventured deeper.

"Sam?" she called.

I'm here.

She looked around then jumped to find him a few feet behind her, petting the fawn.

"You move so quiet," she said, not yet accustomed to the sight of the towering creature.

I am part of the forest.

"So do you just follow me around all day?"

No, human. Sam gave one of his chortled laughs. *I appear when I want you to find me, like you did.*

"Oh. Decker said you don't talk to many people."

Only those I must when I must. Sam held out a leather necklace with a tiny, clear stone. *This will protect you.*

"From what?" she asked, taking it.

The danger around you.

Summer looked up at him. "What danger?"

There are people interested in harming you. This is so they can't hurt you.

"The Dark," she breathed. "It's not Decker, is it?"

No.

"Good." Summer sighed, unaware of how much she wanted it not to be until her chest loosened enough for her to breathe deeply again. "What do you do out here all day? Do you have any friends?"

There are many of us. We monitor the balance.

"Sam, is Decker ... bad?"

You are troubled by such simple thoughts.

Summer flushed. She put on the necklace.

Humans are neither good nor bad. They are filled with choices they've yet to make and those they've already made.

"Okay, fine." She rolled her eyes. "Be as vague as everyone else."

You must decide for yourself about the Master of Fire and Night. Meanwhile, I'll worry about good and evil not destroying the world. His words were spoken with gentle humor and accompanied by a chortle. *You would be quite a pair, one pure set of all the elements.*

"Not if I go to hell for it," she said with determination. "Well, I'm going to dinner."

You are young to worry over your immortality. You have many choices to make yet. He stepped aside and motioned back the way she'd come.

"Thank you for the necklace," she said. She picked her way through a thatch of huckleberry bushes past him. "I'll be careful. I'm from the worst orphanage in LA, so I doubt anything here is going to be half as bad."

He will protect you.

"Who?" she asked, turning.

Sam was gone. Summer snorted. She made her way towards the road and walked down it, trailed by the deer. She liked the strange half-man, half-beast that appeared at odd times, because seeing him made her feel almost normal.

By the time she put Tarzan back in her room, the rest of the teens at the school had gathered at the long table. Seating was unassigned, though she noticed there were cliques of people who sat together. Her gaze went to Beck, who was speaking to one of the other boys. Dawn and the three who had gone shopping with her sat at one end. Summer usually waited until everyone was seated before taking the last empty chair. This evening, Biji waved her over and patted the chair beside her.

Summer smiled at the small girl, who spoke to another girl with thick glasses named Ana. Summer circled the table to sit down, surprised to see Decker directly across from her. She looked at Biji, who grinned. Seating herself, Summer tried hard not to look at the Dark twin but found herself drawn to him.

He met her gaze briefly before looking away. The initial exchange over, Summer relaxed and focused on her food. The first course—salad and soup—came and went, leaving her drooling over what the main course would be. The waiter began setting out the main course.

"Watching Summer eat is the best part of dinner."

Summer heard her name mentioned down the table and glanced up. Dawn was giggling and looking at her, the two girls on either side of her also staring at Summer. Summer's face grew warm. She looked at the half chicken and vegetables the waiter put before her. Instead of holding it

119

with one hand and prying off the meat with a fork, she watched Biji from the corner of her eye.

Biji used fork and knife to slice pieces of meat off the chicken. Summer carefully tried to mimic her movements, sending the vegetables careening off the edges of her plate at the awkward movements. She stopped to eat the veggies then tackled the chicken again. She tried sawing off the top of a chicken leg to free the meat from the cartilage before resorting to brute force. Suddenly, the joint snapped off and sailed down the table.

Dawn and her friends burst into laughter. Biji appeared startled, and Summer stared. Frustrated, she was about to give up and grab the chicken with both hands. Someone's foot settled against hers under the table. She started to shift away when she recognized the magick flowing into her.

She looked at Decker, who was in discussion with the Dark girl beside him. He didn't move, and neither did Summer. Like when they danced, her body seemed to know what to do whenever he touched her. She tried her chicken again, pleased when her hands worked the knife and fork as expertly as Biji.

The rest of her dinner passed with no more embarrassment. Decker didn't even acknowledge her until he pushed his plate away to rise. His foot moved away, the flow of his magick ceasing. Summer glanced up, catching his eye.

"*Thank you,*" she mouthed.

He lifted his chin in response, dark eyes lingering on her before he turned away finally. Summer watched him go, joined by the other Dark teens in the foyer.

"You totally have a crush on him," Biji said.

"I don't. But he's a nice guy," Summer said.

"Nice? Right."

Summer smiled to herself, touched by his thoughtfulness.

"Can I see Tarzan again?" Biji asked.

"Sure."

They left the dining room together and ascended to Summer's room. Tarzan was dozing and raised his head when they entered. Summer turned on the light. It was past dusk, and the light of bonfires in the backyard made shadows dance on the walls.

"Do you sleep with him?" Biji asked.

"Yeah. He kicks me at night."

"He's so cute!"

Summer smiled as Biji sat down and patted the animal. She prepped the bottle Amber had brought her and handed it to Biji. The Indian girl giggled. As much milk ended up on her as in Tarzan's mouth, and the fawn licked up what he'd missed.

"You really do have a deer."

Summer glanced up at Dawn's voice, her smile fading. The blond girl pushed the door to her room open, trailed by one of her friends. Biji scowled openly at Dawn, who ignored her.

"He's so sweet," Dawn cooed, kneeling beside the bed to peer at the deer. "Tarzan is an awful name, though."

"I like it," Biji said promptly.

"What do you feed him?" Dawn asked Summer.

"Milk. And he goes out to eat grass and berries during the day," Summer replied, troubled by the girl's presence after her comment at dinner.

"He's so little," Dawn's friend said. "You can't let him out alone, can you?"

"Not yet," Summer replied. "He's too young to be without his mother. Maybe in another month or two, he can go find a new herd to join."

Tarzan chewed on Dawn's hair, and Dawn tugged it free. Her friend giggled, and Biji muttered under her breath.

"Okay, I'm ready," Dawn said and straightened. "There's nothing to do in this godforsaken place. We're going out back."

"You could sleep with a few more boys," Biji responded.

Dawn gave her a dirty look. "Summer, you're always more than welcome to join us."

"Why, so you can make fun of her, like you do when she's not around?" Biji demanded, rising. "You'll just make jerky out of Tarzan. You need to go, Dawn."

Summer stared at the small girl, surprised.

"Whatever," Dawn replied. "She's only jealous because I never invited her shopping or anywhere like I did you, Summer."

"Good night!" Biji snapped.

Dawn rolled her eyes again and left.

"What a bitch," Biji said as soon as Dawn was gone.

Summer laughed. "You really don't like her!"

"Nope. She's no good for you and no good for Tarzan," Biji said. "I know these things. And I've heard how she talks about you behind your back. I wasn't going to say anything but you're just too nice."

"I'm used to people saying things about me," Summer said. "It doesn't bother me, Biji."

"It bothers me."

Summer stroked the deer's head, marveling at how soft its fur was.

"Hello." The note of awe in Biji's voice replaced her anger.

"Hello."

Summer looked up at Decker's voice. Dawn had left her door open, and Decker stood in the doorway. He was tall and wide enough to fill the door frame.

"I came to see how Tarzan is doing," he said.

"You can come in," Biji said eagerly.

"Thanks." He stayed where he was, gaze on the small deer.

Summer was as mesmerized by him as Biji, not expecting to find his draw even stronger at night than it was in the day. His dark, soft eyes were like the night. He met her gaze at last. Summer crossed her arms as a shiver ran through her.

"Are you going to the dance?" Biji asked him.

"I don't dance," he replied with his normal brusqueness.

"I can teach you."

"No."

"So you really aren't going? It's the last dance before the school year starts."

"No."

Summer looked away to keep from smiling. Biji was determined.

"What if you could dance with Summer?" Biji pushed.

"Biji!" Summer exclaimed. Her stomach fluttered at the idea, but she didn't want him answering. If he said no, she'd be crushed, even though she had a date.

"Let him answer, Summer!"

Summer looked at him again, cringing internally.

"I might," he said finally.

Summer's breath caught at his direct look.

"So you can go to the dance and dance with Summer then me," Biji decided.

"Biji, you know——" Summer hissed.

"Just because you already have a date doesn't mean you can't dance with someone else," Biji returned.

"You already have a date." The note of cooling in Decker's voice was plain. He crossed his arms.

"Sort of," Summer replied. "I'm sorry, Decker."

"I hope he can dance half as well as we might."

She flushed at the quiet words.

"Well, he should," Biji said. "He's your brother."

Decker stepped back from the door, his quick footfalls on the stairwell down to the first floor making her wince.

"Oh, Biji," Summer murmured.

"That was kind of weird, wasn't it?" Biji said. "We almost got him to go, and I almost got a dance in his dreamy arms!" She hugged herself and danced around the room.

Summer couldn't help feeling as if the rug was pulled out from under her. Her gaze went to the suitcase, where she'd placed the notes Beck had left for her the past couple of days. They'd thrilled her at first, but she felt no comfort from them now. Not when she knew Decker had wanted to dance with her.

He'd probably never show up to their morning lessons again. The thought of dancing without him made her fidget.

Chapter Eight

DECKER WASN'T SURE which shocked him more: that his brother had unknowingly moved into his territory or that Summer would choose someone else over him, even knowing she felt their magick when they danced. He paused when he reached the first floor. More than his pride was bruised. Maybe this was better. He hadn't wanted to drag Summer into his world.

The thought had never crossed his mind that Summer didn't feel for him as he did for her, that she wanted nothing to do with him. He stepped into the cool night. Every day, the sensation of darkness grew around him, within him. It was comforting as it flowed through his body yet caused his headaches to grow during the day. He was becoming more and more sensitive to those around him, a necessity for one who must track evil.

Disturbed, he went to the square out back. The bonfires were lit. His brother was absent, probably in their room.

Decker returned to their room and froze as he opened the door. Beck and Dawn were half-naked on Beck's bed in a make-out frenzy.

"Later, Decker!" Beck all but shouted.

"It's my room. Get out, Dawn."

The lust-struck lovers both looked startled at his low growl. He hadn't meant it to come out so harsh. Or maybe he did. Beck was good-natured enough to believe Dawn if she said she was on the pill, and Dawn was conniving enough to lie to him to get knocked up and tap their trust funds.

After a moment, she grabbed her clothes and dressed calmly, looking up at him with a smile as she left. He locked the door behind her.

"Dude, what the hell?" Beck demanded, tugging his shorts back on.

"You two didn't break up?"

"Why does everyone think we did?"

"Maybe because you asked Summer to the dance with you."

"Oh, god. This again." Beck rose and opened the top drawer of his nightstand. "Dawn was playing a joke on her, and it got out of hand. She keeps writing me notes and seems convinced I'm going to the dance with her. Dawn's tried to tell her a million times it's just some sick delusion."

"Summer's writing you notes?" Decker asked, taken aback.

"Look at these. Every time I come back to the room, there's another one." Beck said and picked up a stack of lined paper covered with flowery handwriting. "There's like, twenty of these things."

Decker took them, his heart at his feet. He couldn't imagine Summer doing such a thing, but then again, he didn't know much about her, aside from how he felt. His insides were cold as he took the notes.

"What did Dawn do?" he asked, perplexed.

"She pranked Summer. Pretended to be me, wrote Summer a note and asked her to the dance. Things got out of control after that. She came to me finally and admitted it."

"You ever think Dawn wrote these, too?"

"It's not her handwriting," Beck snapped. "And yes, I checked. I know you don't trust her, and I trust your judgment, even if I don't like to hear it."

Decker looked up, not expecting his brother to admit to trusting anything he said, especially about Dawn. Beck looked troubled but said nothing. His words about Summer made Decker nauseous.

"At least you didn't ask her out," he managed and sat with the letters in his hand.

"You like her?" Beck asked, surprised. "She doesn't seem like your type."

"What's my type, Beck?"

"Alexa."

Decker snorted and stretched out on his bed. He began to read the letters and got through four before he set them down. Professions of love, sexual references ... he was expecting quotes by Shakespeare, not something that read like it was pulled out of a teen magazine.

"Weird, aren't they?" Beck asked. "Goes to show you never know who the psychos are."

It can't be her, Decker replied silently.

"So, no, I'm not going with her to the dance. If you can take that twisted bitch off my hands, I'd appreciate it."

Decker stared at the ceiling.

127

"On the topic of twisted bitches, Alexa was looking for you," Beck added. "We both have our girl issues. Did you break up with her or something?"

"Yeah."

"That would explain the dead bird she left at the door. Is that some kind of curse or something?"

"Pretty much." Decker didn't want to deal with Alexa at all.

"That's all I need."

"Your life seems pretty stable. What's wrong?" Decker asked, twisting his head to see his twin.

"There's a rumor about Dawn going around."

"Let me guess. She cheated on you."

"You heard it?"

"No, idiot. She cheated on me, remember?"

"Guess I didn't think about that. You guys didn't date long anyway."

Decker said nothing. His attention returned to the letters. He read another one, growing less and less convinced. He'd never seen any of Summer's writing, but she appeared too smart to misspell works like *heaven*. The girl who dutifully attended her fawn, had one friend, and rarely spoke didn't seem capable of the over-the-top language in the letters.

"This just—"

A knock at their door made him lower the letters. Beck was almost fully dressed again and crossed to the door as he buckled his belt.

Alexa stood in the doorway. Beck glanced at Decker, who rose.

"I'll go for a walk," Beck said, moving around her.

Decker took in Alexa's features. She looked determined, and there was a gleam in her gaze he couldn't interpret. She stepped into the room and closed the door behind her. Her one hand was shoved in her pocket. Without speaking, she moved towards him and pulled her fist out, flinging something at his face.

Decker coughed as what looked like black glitter sprayed him. His body absorbed the Dark magick of the spell, unaffected.

"That stuff doesn't work on me," he told her, wiping it off his face. "What is it?"

"Love spell," she said and frowned. She searched his gaze. "Decker, the time we spent together was the best time of my life. Please, please tell me we can try again."

"No."

"I'll do anything, Decker."

"Alexa, I shouldn't have taken advantage of you. I'm sorry. I really am," he said with feeling. "I didn't think twice and should have."

"I heard Matilda tell Amber last night I might be the one who is meant to be your partner, to help you through your transition," she said. "I can do it, Decker."

"Matilda's wrong."

Loss then anger crossed Alexa's features. She paced. Decker eased away, sensing she was ready to explode.

"What if I'm pregnant?" she demanded.

"We used condoms."

"Condoms don't always work."

"Look, Alexa, I know what you're—"

"So you just woke up and decided you were done with me?" She stopped and stared at him. "There's someone else, isn't there?"

"There's no one."

"Guys don't just walk away from me, Decker! I've never had anyone—"

"It's over, Alexa!" he said more loudly. "I'm about to become a monster, and I won't drag you into it."

She frowned. "Is that what this is about? You're afraid of what happens in two weeks?"

"I'm terrified. But aside from that, I won't put anyone else in danger."

"Oh, Decker." She softened again. "I'll stand by you. I promise."

Frustrated, he tried to think of something diplomatic to say to make her leave him alone.

"You don't have to worry. I'll always—"

"No, Alexa," he said at last. "No. We're through. I made a mistake and now it's done. I'm sorry if I hurt your feelings."

Her eyes fell to the notes written in pink pen in his hand. Before he could react, she snatched the letters. He reached for them, but she skirted him.

"There is someone else!" Her features twisted again into rage.

"*My dearest love,*" she started. She gave him a warning glare then read fast, turning it over to see who signed it. "Summer. You're ditching me for Summer?"

"No. I'm not ditching you for anyone. These letters—"

"That short, fat bitch with big boobs. You're leaving me for her." Alexa wasn't listening.

"She's not short, fat or a bitch!" Decker snapped and snatched the letters. "You're not listening—"

Wounded and angry, Alexa looked up at him. "You may be immune to my spells, but she's not!" She snatched the doorknob and yanked the door open.

Decker planted a hand above her head and slammed it closed. His body was tense with fury and magick again. It boiled just beneath his level of control, wanting to be free.

"If you so much as look at her wrong, you will be the first I track down after I turn eighteen. You understand me?" he whispered.

Alexa hunched her shoulders. She wrenched the door open and faced him when she'd made it safely onto the landing. He couldn't do anything with the bonfires full of teens a few feet away.

"You can't protect her all the time, Master of Fire and Night," she hissed.

Decker slammed the door, his head pounding. The sounds of the others' souls were even louder this night. He paced, but the clamor only grew louder. He wanted to explode and pulled his door open.

He ran into the forest, not caring that the branches lashed him as he went. He ran until the sounds of the others were too faint for his throbbing head, and he dropped to his knees in a small clearing.

"Sam!" he shouted into the air. "Come out, Sam!"

He heard no response for a long moment and slumped. His headache eased, and he flung his head back to see the stars. He'd gone so far as to put up constellations above his bed at the cabin—where he spent the weekends and many nights—after talking to Summer about stars. He recognized a few of the constellations and breathed the cool night air deeply until his nerves calmed.

The Master of Night is distressed, Sam's voice came to him at last. *What troubles you, Master?*

"Everything," Decker whispered.

The yeti emerged from the dark forest and sat in front of Decker. Its auburn fur glowed like fire in the moonlight.

"You're the only one I can talk to, Sam."

It was the same for your mother before she took her oath to the Dark. The world grows both darker and lighter. The sensations hurt, but you will get used to them.

"If you say so."

I do say so, boy, Sam said with his chortle-laugh.

"I don't want this. I don't want to go mad like Bartholomew. I don't want to spend my life so far from the Light."

Your profession is a noble one. You serve the Light in a different way, by enforcing the Dark Laws upon those who threaten the Light.

"I know this. But I feel so ..."

Alone. Frightened.

"Yes to both. I don't feel ready for this."

No one ever does.

Decker rubbed his face.

Do you ever wonder why your bloodline was chosen for this honor?

"You mean the curse? No. Mother said the curse was placed on us two thousand years ago."

It is not a curse, Sam corrected firmly. *It is an honor. Your bloodline was chosen because of its purity and strength. Your ancestors faced evil unlike any this world has ever known since. They defeated it and swore the greatest of all oaths: to continue to protect the balance by sacrificing themselves and their children.*

Decker listened to the creature's voice, relaxing.

You are stronger than the others. Those of your blood have always been stronger than the others.

"I don't feel it." Decker sighed.

Trust me.

"I do, Sam."

How is your brother?

132

"Good. Our mother took us both out to show us what she does. What I'll do in two weeks." He shuddered. "It changed things between me and Beck."

You two have always been close. She still mourns for her twin.

"Yeah. I would, too."

And Summer?

Decker looked up, surprised the creature would ask. Sam met his gaze, waiting with the patience of a creature that had lived through thousands of human years.

"She's safe," Decker said at last. "I don't know what else to say."

You need to trust yourself.

"Seriously, Sam? I'm about to become the devil. I don't trust anything about myself."

You need each other. By now, even someone as stubborn as you can see that. Sam chuckled.

Decker looked up at the stars again. He knew it. But he wasn't going to drag her into hell with him. He closed his eyes, imagining what it would be like if she was there, touching him, quelling the chaos in his head and body.

He hadn't wanted to go dance with her in the morning, not after she chose Beck over him. He didn't know what was going on with the letters, but he suspected Dawn was involved somehow. Summer wouldn't …

Then again, she chose his brother over him, even after their time dancing together.

"I don't know what to think, Sam," he said.

Don't think. Feel. And enjoy your time before your transition.

"Whatever, Sam."

Whatever! Sam laughed, a booming guffaw. *I love this word. It is my favorite from your generation.*

133

Decker smiled, unable to keep a straight face when Sam looked so awkward laughing. His thoughts went to Summer again. Whatever was going on, she didn't deserve to get hurt.

He stayed in the forest with Sam, talking, until almost dawn. Soon, the creature would be the only one he could talk to.

Summer slept poorly and was antsy all morning, until the moment she dreaded finally came. The dance class finished up, and the girls left. Jessie remained. Amber joined them, dressed in yoga pants and a loose shirt, and another woman entered. Summer recognized the instructor of the Dark students, Matilda, who wore all black yoga pants and a snug shirt. Her ballerina body was something even Dawn would be jealous of, and Summer gazed at her for a long moment.

"Jessie, I didn't realize you had other plans today," Summer said, turning at last.

Decker was five minutes late. He wasn't coming.

"Nonsense. They heard how successful our dance classes were and decided to come for some tips," Jessie answered. "Let's start with some basics. Amber, Matty, line up beside me. Summer on the end."

The women obeyed. Summer glanced at the clock again, heartbroken Decker had decided not to come after last night. She struggled to focus on Jessie's instructions. Salsa music played loudly. Amber seemed to get it but Matty didn't, and neither did Summer, without her partner.

Fifteen minutes late, Decker finally appeared in the doorway. There were circles under his eyes and pine needles stuck in the creases of his clothing. Summer stopped in place, thrilled he came, even if she had rejected him the day before.

134

"'Bout time. Other side of Matty!" Jessie called. "These two are worse than you and Summer!"

Decker said nothing but took his place on the other end of the line. Jessie barked more tips before pairing them up, Amber and Summer, Matilda and Decker. Summer grinned as Amber trampled her feet with laughed apologies. They struggled through a whole song before Jessie assigned them new partners: Summer and Matilda, Amber and Decker. The Dark instructor was neither as free with her smiles nor as forgiving of her own missteps.

"Decker and Summer, Amber and Matty!" Jessie called between songs.

Decker didn't hesitate to reach for her this time, and Summer fell into step with him, a shiver working through her at the flood of his heat and magick. Sam had called him the Master of Fire and Night. Summer could feel both swirl through her. The lively music and dance steps made her feel alive. Even Decker smiled as he spun her one way, then another before folding her into his arms for a quick dip. Fire tore through her at the full body contact.

Breathless from the dance, Summer welcomed the next, slow song.

"I didn't think you'd come today," she said when she'd caught her breath.

"I didn't either," Decker admitted. He was troubled by something. "Maybe you shouldn't—"

"And pause!" Jessie said. "You two have far outstripped these novices." She motioned to the two instructors.

Summer withdrew from Decker.

"I'm going to spend some time with my new students. The dance is tomorrow night, and I'm on vacation tomorrow. You'll do fine together," Jessie said to the two of them. "You two, shoo! I'll see you Monday."

Summer picked up her shoes and left. She didn't hear Decker following until he touched her arm in the hallway. Turning, she couldn't help stepping closer to him to feel the shared sense of magick as they did when they danced.

"Summer, I think you should go to the dance with me," he said.

"I can't, Decker. I told your brother I'd go with him."

"Can you ... *feel* what's between us?" he asked.

"Decker," she said softly and moved away until their contact broke. "I've enjoyed our lessons but ..." ... *this terrifies me,* she finished silently.

"But what? They told you what I am, didn't they." Irritation crossed his features. "My brother is just going to break your heart tomorrow night."

"You shouldn't say that," she said, frowning. "And no one told me anything about you."

"You're saying this is your choice?"

She hesitated, gazing up into his dark eyes. Her heart said no, she belonged with him. Fear won out, and she was silent.

"Very well." He stepped around her and strode down the hallway and out the front door.

Summer watched him, torn. The letters from Beck were so sweet. Not only had she already agreed to a date, Beck had confessed his interest with her, while Decker had said little. She went to her room, troubled.

Biji was waiting for her, seated outside with her smartphone. She glanced up with a smile, and Summer pushed away her dark thoughts. She opened the door so they could play with Tarzan.

136

Chapter Nine

DESPITE HER ATTEMPTS to think of anything but the dance, Summer found herself distracted up until it was time to get ready. She hadn't seen Decker since their last dance, and she couldn't help the doubt that grew in her. Decker had never said anything about liking her, but he'd helped her at dinner and danced with her.

Beck hadn't done those things. And yet, the thought of dancing with Beck the way she danced with Decker thrilled her.

"No, no, you have to wear your hair down," Biji instructed.

Summer glanced at her friend. Biji wore an exotic Indian sari in brilliant oranges and reds. Her long, dark hair had been brushed to a sheen and rippled like black silk.

"You look like a doll," Summer said, admiring her friend.

Biji beamed. "Maybe Decker will go and maybe he'll dance with me."

"You have a one-track mind!" Summer laughed.

"You look great, Summer," Biji said, hunching beside her to see into the mirror on the back of the door. "Except your hair."

Summer looked at herself, unconvinced. She'd cleaned the soft pink dress. It was a baby-doll style that emphasized her breasts and slender waist before flowing over her hips. Washing it had caused it to shrink more than she liked. The hem of the dress was halfway up her thighs. She'd worn her sandals, the only shoes she had that didn't clash too loudly with the dress. They were old and looked it. Her gaze swept over her body and lingered on her shoes.

Biji had painted her toe and fingernails a bright pink.

"You think it should be down?" Summer asked.

"Definitely." Biji pulled a chair from the corner and placed it before the mirror. She grabbed Summer's brush and comb.

Summer sat. Her hair was still damp. Biji unwound it from the tight bun Summer had put it in before working out the knots with her comb.

"You have hairspray?" Biji asked.

"No."

"I might have some."

Summer watched Biji in the mirror as she dug through a large handbag. It looked pricey, like the bags Summer saw displayed in the windows of the expensive stores at the mall. Biji pulled out a travel-size hairspray and proceeded to redo Summer's hair into soft waves.

"One more thing then we're ready," Biji said. She rifled through her bag again and pulled out a thick silver belt. "I thought your dress needed something else."

"Why are you being so nice?" Summer asked, struck by her friend's actions.

"That's what friends do," Biji said nonchalantly, wrapping the belt around her body.

Summer's throat tightened.

"Haven't you ever ..." Biji stopped. "You've never had a friend before?"

"Not a nice one."

Biji laughed.

"Thank you, Biji," Summer said. "I've never had a friend like you before. This place is like a dream to me. I can't believe I'm here."

"I'm glad you're here. I can't imagine your life if you think dealing with Dawn is good," Biji said. "Ready?"

"No."

"Come on! You've got a date waiting for you!"

Summer smiled. She looked at herself again, patted Tarzan then trailed Biji down the stairs. Her heart sank some to see Dawn and her friends waiting in the lobby for the van. Dawn and her friends wore their expensive, revealing dresses and high heels, and they carried small evening bags. Their make-up was heavy and flawless.

Summer crossed her arms, feeling plain next to them in their high fashion. She hadn't thought to put on anything but gloss and mascara, because she didn't have anything else. She looked at Biji for some support. Biji was glaring at Dawn openly. Summer nudged her.

"You look too nice tonight not to smile," she whispered. "Ignore her."

"We are cuter," Biji said grudgingly.

"You are," Summer agreed. "Are you going to—"

"Summer, you look gorgeous," Dawn exclaimed from across the foyer. "I never would've guessed you bought that dress from a yard sale."

The girls with her laughed. Biji stepped forward, red-faced. Summer took her arm.

"Thank you, Dawn. You look beautiful," she said before Biji could retort.

"I knew Beck would like it," Dawn said and smoothed her hands over her hips. "Do you think he will?"

"Um, yes," Summer said uneasily.

"He's my date, you know."

Summer frowned. She was about to retrieve the letters from her room to make sure she hadn't made a mistake when Amber flung the screen door open.

"Ride's here!" she called. "Everyone in."

Dawn and her friends were the first out. Summer hesitated.

"She's just messing with you," Biji told her. "Come on. Beck is a good guy. If he said he's going with you, then he will. She's just jealous."

Summer smiled and let Biji pull her out of the house.

"He did say he was going with you, right?" Biji whispered as they stood in line to enter the van.

"Yes. Well, he wrote it. I haven't actually talked to him."

"What? Are you serious?"

"In the van, girls!" Amber said again.

Biji climbed in and sat beside one of Dawn's friends while Summer sat on the bench two seats ahead of her. Their conversation was silenced. Summer felt a sliver of dread, not for the first time. She gazed out the window as they drove. The dark reminded her of Decker.

She barely recognized the resort when they piled out of the van. It was brilliantly lit, the walkway to the dock hidden between darkness and trees. She could see teens in the main floor of the resort through the windows.

"Let's find Beck," Biji said and grabbed her hand. She tugged Summer into a side entrance and ran up stairs to the main level.

Summer followed. The Dark teens were lined on one side and the Light on the other. Only a few couples ventured onto the dance floor. The edges of the room were dark and the dance floor brightly lit while music throbbed. One wall held buffet tables lined with snacks and punch, and bright decorations had been hung up all over the room.

She wound her way through the Dark teens. A sense reached her, one that told her Decker was close even without seeing him. She glanced around before catching sight of Biji again. The smaller girl was waving at her frantically, standing in front of a small group of Light boys, including Beck.

Summer's heart pounded. She'd all but memorized his notes and recited them as she approached. Biji tapped his arm, and he turned, taking them both in with smiles. His hair was combed, his teal eyes making Summer's knees weak. She hadn't seen him in a few days and yet, his appearance didn't impact her as much as Decker's.

"Glad you could make it!" he said to her over the music. "You look great."

"You guys should dance!" Biji said.

Beck glanced around, his hesitance brief. "Sure. Come on, Summer."

Summer couldn't help feeling even more triumphant over Dawn. Biji was right; Dawn was jealous. Summer took Beck's hand when he offered it and ventured onto the dance floor with him.

She felt none of his magick, and her first attempt to keep up with the dance moves failed. She looked at one of the other girls and tried to mimic the movements. Her own lightness on her feet helped keep the situation from getting too awkward, but she wasn't comfortable.

"I got your notes," she said, looking up at Beck.

"Notes," he said. "Okay."

"They were nice," she said. "It's the reason I came."

His brow furrowed. "I meant to talk to you about that."

"Sure."

"I, uh, got your notes, too."

Summer waited, puzzled by his words. She'd written no notes to him, only passed back the first one, as it instructed.

"And the video," he said, face reddening. "You look very nice in your ... um, but uh, I'm kind of—"

"What video?" she asked.

"I don't think you meant to forward it to everyone, but we all got it," he said. "Look, I'm flattered, I really am—"

"What video?"

"The one of you undressing. Good footage, of course, but probably not something you should've put on YouTube."

Summer stopped in place. Beck looked nervous. A roaring was filling her ears, and her face felt hot enough to explode.

"I'm with Dawn, so I'm sorry I can't really, you know, hook up," he said. "I'm really sorry. You're a great girl. And I have to say, the video was like, wow. We were looking at it again on the ride over. It's kind of cool that you sleep naked."

"Who all saw it?" she managed.

"Everyone. The link went out to all of us on our school email accounts."

"Hi, guys," Dawn said, approaching them. She struck a pose then made a kissy-face at Beck, who pecked her on the lips. "Don't you like Summer's dress? She found it in a trash can and fixed it up."

"It's, ah, nice."

"Did you tell her?"

"Yes, we were just talking about it," Beck said. "Only one girl for me."

Dawn batted her eyelashes at him and maneuvered between them.

"I'm sorry, but he's taken, Summer. No more videos, okay?"

Summer stepped back, unable to register exactly what happened. She looked around, feeling cold. All the guys in the room were staring at her, a few snickering. She felt exposed standing in the middle of the dance floor. Not only had everyone seen her very public snub from Beck, but they'd all seen her *naked*.

Someone set her up. Staring at the two dancing, she couldn't help thinking it was Dawn.

Summer moved out of the spotlight and bumped into one guy then strode towards the door. Everyone seemed to be staring at her, ridiculing her. Her tears held until she reached the outdoors. The patio was open and empty, and she sat down in one chair, devastated.

In one night, her paradise had been destroyed. No one would want anything to do with her after this! Amber would send her away, back to the orphanage, for a video she had nothing to do with. Even if they didn't, how could she live in a place where everyone was laughing at her?

143

"Hey. Uh, can I ask you something?"

She wiped her tears away hastily at the sound of Beck's voice and rose to face him.

"You didn't send the video, did you?"

She shook her head.

"Or the notes?"

"No."

He appeared troubled. "That sucks. I owe you an apology, then."

"It's okay. I'm used to people messing with me." Summer crossed her arms, chilled in the evening air.

"I've got a list of girls a mile long who want to dance with me, but if you want to go back inside, you'll be the first," he offered. "I don't know what happened, but I'll make it up to you." A note in his voice told her he suspected he knew what happened.

"No thanks," she said. "I'll probably just take a shuttle ride back to the dorms."

"Well, if you change your mind, come on back inside."

"Thanks, Beck."

He flashed his famous smile and turned away, disappearing into the resort. While she appreciated his words, any affection she felt for him was gone. He'd all but helped humiliate her.

She always ended up alone. Summer gazed at the forest, hurting more than she could remember. The two weeks at the new school had lulled her into believing this time would be different. She'd lowered her guard, begun to accept that she might fit in here. She'd even taken her jewelry box out of her suitcase and set it on the dresser.

I should've gone with Decker. Her instincts had told her as much. But even he might've seen the video. She wasn't sure how she'd face him, if so.

Heart aching, Summer sniffed back more tears and walked towards the dock. The forest was alive with night sounds around her, the air even colder next to the lake. She sat on the edge of the dock, hugging her knees in an attempt to keep warm.

"Shouldn't you be dancing with Beck?"

She squeezed her eyes closed at Decker's voice. His step was light on the wood of the dock.

"Why are you crying?" The sarcasm left his voice.

"I owe you an apology, Decker."

"Don't bother. You made your choice."

Summer twisted to see him a few feet away. His magick brushed by her, comforting with its dark-heat sensations. She rose, and he turned to leave.

"Decker, I mean it. I made a mistake."

"I take it something bad happened. I'm not going to be a back-up plan."

"I don't want you to be," she said. "I'm not asking anything of you. Just apologizing."

He was silent, though he didn't leave.

"And I hope you didn't see the video," she added quietly. "Did you?"

"Yeah."

More tears rose. Decker's magick was just out of reach, and she was alone again, cold and alone.

"You've been the only person who's been decent to me. You and Biji. I'll miss you when they send me away," she whispered.

"They won't send you away."

"They always do."

He faced her, his features hidden by darkness.

"Would you dance with me, Decker? One last dance?" she ventured, wanting to feel his magick through her again.

"No."

His rejection crushed her more than Beck's, more than Dawn's carefully executed humiliation. Summer's throat was tight. She nodded in understanding, wishing she could go back to the hallway the day before and accept his offer of taking her to the dance.

Chapter Ten

DECKER HAD NEVER felt like more of a dick than he did standing there, knowing how upset she was. He'd suspected Dawn or someone else was playing a joke. At first, he felt vindicated seeing Summer cry. He was angry at everything, even her, the victim of a horrible joke.

And then he thought of his sweet Summer in pain and was crushed by the idea he was partially responsible for causing it. She looked beautiful, glowing like a flower among rocks. Her tears glimmered in the starlight. He should leave her, walk into the jaws of hell alone, and spare them both what pain might come.

He couldn't. Right now, she stood before him, offering herself, if he'd take her. Her touch was the only thing that could calm him. He wanted ... *needed* to feel her.

"I want more than one dance, Summer," he said in a hushed voice. "I can't explain it."

Her breath caught. She looked up at him. His words hung in the air between them. He held out his hand. Summer looked at it then at him.

"You want to dance here?" she asked, taking it. "There's no music."

Decker swept her into his arms. "We don't need music."

They didn't. Her touch made him shudder, and their bodies synced as they did every time they danced. The music originated from their entwined souls. The blue flames of his magick traveled over her at each point where their bodies touched. Like a switch turning off, the chaos in his mind disappeared. His body relaxed, and he sensed her body yield as well.

"You're not talking about dancing," she said.

"No, I'm not," he replied, heart quickening. He was lost in her dark gaze and soft scent, both girly and earthy. "I'm talking about this, whatever this is. I wasn't sure you felt it."

"I do. I just ... I'm afraid of what it means."

"You'll fear it more when I tell you what I am."

She tensed but didn't look away or try to move away. Pressed together, their bodies kept the innate rhythm.

"What?" she asked at last.

Decker drew a breath. Fear trickled through him at the thought of her rejection. He couldn't live with himself if she walked away. He couldn't live with himself if he tricked her into being with him, and she found out in two weeks what that really meant. She'd hate him.

"Decker, what?"

"When Beck and I turn eighteen, he becomes the Master of Light, and I become the Master of ..."

She stumbled and stopped in place, staring up at him. Her breathing grew fast and erratic, the pulse in her wrist beating like a machine gun against his hand.

"Fire and Night," she finished in a voice almost too quiet to hear.

He nodded, throat tightening.

Her gaze went to the blue fire traveling up and down her arms. Decker looked at it as well, unable to stop the creep of his magick into her body. It acted as if they were one body, not two, and wouldn't stay inside him. She said nothing. Decker shifted away and released her, expecting the rejection to follow. The effect she had on him faded without disappearing completely.

"I'm sorry, Summer," he whispered. "I understand."

He turned to walk away. The chaos and fury returned to his head. He walked a few steps and was about to run for the darkness of the forest when her cool hand touched his arm. Decker stopped without turning.

"I think you were trying to ask me if I wanted to be with you, even if you are so Dark," she said, her voice sounding breathless. "You didn't let me answer, Decker."

He closed his eyes, bracing himself.

"Yes, Decker. My answer is yes. I don't even know if that was your question, but that's my answer."

He was still a moment, not registering her words. Summer circled him until she stood toe-to-toe with him. He felt her butterfly kiss on his lips and opened his eyes, the truth registering. Her dark eyes were in turmoil, the tears like diamonds on the pale silk of her face. She smiled at him. He released the breath he held and wiped the diamonds from her cheeks.

Decker's hands moved over her arms and took her hands. He wasn't sure what to say, if he should listen to his joyful heart or the fear and dread in his stomach. That she accepted him even knowing what he'd become thrilled him.

"This is like a dream," he said. "Any minute I'll wake up and you'll be gone forever."

"You sound like me," she said, smile widening. "It's no dream, Decker. I want to be with you."

"I swear I'll protect you from whatever I become," he whispered.

"Before I came here, no one could accept all of me, because my magick made me so different. I won't do that to you," she replied. "When you care about someone, you accept all of them."

Decker wrapped his arms around her and sighed, touched by the words. He'd seen pain in her gaze when she spoke them and knew what it was like to be reviled for being different. She'd been molded by years of the same treatment. Beneath the shy exterior, she was tough. She'd survived the world alone as a freak among humans.

Maybe, just maybe, he didn't have to be alone after all. Or maybe, this was the last-ditch effort of a desperate fool.

"In two weeks—" he started.

"I don't care. We feel right. Let's just ... feel right." She turned her face up to him. "Okay?"

Decker kissed her and pulled her harder against him. Even her lips gave off bursts of magick that lit his blood on fire. He didn't deserve her, but he'd do what she said and let himself feel the joy bubbling. They'd take it one day at a time. Suddenly, two weeks seemed much longer, if he could spend every day with the beautiful girl in his arms.

Summer dreamt she was still in his arms. When she woke, the idea she had a boyfriend almost seemed too far-fetched. Tarzan was up and pacing. It was Saturday, which meant no classes. Summer rose and showered, her insides almost shaking with anticipation of seeing Decker again.

She'd slept fully clothed then dressed in the bathroom. It was too dark to ransack her room for the camera spying on her when she got home, but she did it now. Summer swung open the door to her closet and searched the few clothes she had hanging up. She'd put her sandals on the floor of the closet, and there were empty shoeboxes on the top shelf of the closet when she arrived.

Dragging a chair to the closet, she stepped up on it to reach the shoeboxes. The first one she shook was empty. The second contained something in it. Summer opened it to see the small camera. It was a wireless camera with a light glowing red on the top.

She moved to sit on her bed and fiddled with it until the battery compartment opened. The light went out when the batteries fell out.

"Summer, you awake?" Amber's voice made her look up.

"Yes."

Amber opened the door, her hair wet and piled on top of her hair. She wore simple jeans and a T-shirt.

"I wanted to talk to you about something really fast, before breakfast," Amber said.

"Sure," Summer said, stomach sinking.

"There's a video circulating with you in it."

151

Summer flushed. She hadn't wanted to think about it. She put the camera and batteries in the shoebox and held it out to Amber.

"I found this in my closet."

"I didn't think you'd done it," Amber said. "The IT guys purged it from the system, but I think it's too late at this point. But I have to ask, did you email it to everyone?"

"No, Amber."

"I believe you. Just doing my part here," Amber said. "Any idea who did?"

Summer shook her head.

"That I don't believe," Amber said. "You protecting someone?"

"I don't want any issues," Summer said.

"I'll deal with whoever it is."

"I've heard that too much in my life. It never happens the way it should."

Amber's features softened, and she sat on the bed beside Summer. The gentle teacher swept a strand of Summer's hair behind her ear.

"Do you like it here?" she asked.

"I've never been anywhere else I love as much as I do here," Summer replied. "I keep waiting to wake up and be back in the orphanage."

"The teachers say you're a good student, and the kids like you. You're a natural here."

"Will I get to stay?" Summer asked, wringing the shirt she wore.

"Yep. We're sending our weekly progress reports to the orphanage. Your director seems pleased you've settled in well here. They'll start sending you a stipend for books and clothes in a week or so. I think it's safe to say you're here to stay, kiddo."

Summer flung her arms around Amber at the news.

"You're a good kid," Amber said, laughing. "You're on the path to the Light. After your birthday in two weeks, you'll be an official member of the Light."

"Thank you, Amber," Summer said. She felt as if something within her released. The fear she carried with her everywhere, that she'd never find a place where she fit in, disappeared.

For the first time since she was four, she had a home. And a boyfriend. And friends and people who weren't afraid of what was inside her. Her humiliation about the video faded.

"Now we just need to unlock your magick before your birthday, or you may not have access to it afterwards. Witchlings are strange like that," Amber said. "Did you talk to our forest friend, Sam?"

Summer nodded as she withdrew. There were tears in her eyes for the second time in two days, but these were tears of happiness.

"Did he give you any advice about opening your magick?"

"Sorta," Summer said. "He said I have to find what makes it sing."

"Good. It's the best that we can explain. Do you have any ideas?"

There was a light tap at her door. Amber released her and crossed to it.

"Hi, Decker. How are you?" she asked cheerfully.

Summer stood nervously.

"Hi, Amber," Decker replied. "I came to get Summer for breakfast."

Amber turned and raised an eyebrow at Summer then smiled. She pulled the door open and reached down to pat the fawn.

"We'll finish this later, Summer. Can you come see me sometime?" she asked.

"Of course," Summer said.

"Have a good breakfast, guys." Amber winked. Decker moved out of her way, and she disappeared into the hallway.

Summer stared at Decker, uncertain what to do or say. Red crept up his face, and he rubbed the back of his head before offering her his hand. She took it, unable to help her grin.

"Are you upset?" he asked, touching her cheek.

"Oh, no," Summer said quickly. She wiped away her tears. "Amber told me I can stay. The orphanage will let me."

"Why wouldn't they let you stay?"

"I've never stayed anywhere for more than a month or two. My um, magick acts out and I usually end up in trouble."

"That's not your fault, though," he replied.

"I know that now. I wish I'd come here instead of the orphanage to begin with."

"It happens to all of us. Amber and Matilda try to find our kind as young as possible, so we have time to learn our skills. I can't believe they missed you." He glanced down at her, his dark eyes warm.

Summer shrugged. "I was moved around so much, I didn't even know where I was."

"You're here now." He squeezed her hand, sending a burst of his magick through her. His confidence floored her. "You want to go for a walk after breakfast?"

"Absolutely."

Her head was swimming with him. She didn't even notice the startled looks those at the breakfast table gave them when they walked in. She ordered what she'd eaten every day: pancakes, eggs, bacon, and orange juice. Decker ordered an egg white omelet and turkey sausage.

"You sure you should be eating so much? I saw the video." One of Dawn's friends giggled as Summer's food arrived. "You could lose a few pounds."

She glanced down the table towards the three girls. They were all there, except Dawn. Decker squeezed her thigh just above the knee under the table, and Summer smiled. Even Dawn and the awful video couldn't keep her down today.

They finished breakfast and left the house, hand-in-hand. They followed the road back toward the bridge Biji had showed her.

"So, what's your story?" Decker asked. "Were you born in an orphanage?"

"No. My family died in a car accident when I was four. My mother had an aunt, but they couldn't find her, so I became a ward of the state," Summer replied. "I spent time in a few foster homes, but my magick kinda made it hard to stay anywhere."

"No siblings or anything?" He was studying her.

"Just me."

"I can't imagine a life like that. Beck drives me crazy, but he's still there for me when I need him."

"What about your parents?" she asked.

"My mother is a Dark witchling, my father a Light. They own a couple of companies and travel a lot." He shrugged. "They're good people. Gave me and Beck a lot of independence growing up."

155

"Must be nice to have a family," she said somewhat wistfully. "A real home."

"I never really thought about it, until you got here. I've never met an orphan before."

"There are a lot of kids without homes. Sometimes I felt lucky I was in the state system and not on the streets. But sometimes, it was just like a prison."

"What did you do for fun?"

"Not much. I listened to music and just read. What about you?"

"I play all kinds of sports, ski, hike. I made the state championships for swimming. Never been into music too much but I like dancing with you."

Summer looked up at him to see he was gazing down at her. His direct look made her lower belly warm.

"I really like it," he added.

"Me, too," she said. "What is … this?" She held up their joined hands. Blue flames from his magick flickered around them.

"I have no idea," he admitted. "I knew it the day I met you. I've never felt anything like it."

"It's wonderful."

"It makes me want to touch you more and more." He smiled, the first she'd seen, and wrapped his arms around her, pulling her in for a hug.

Summer's whole body sang at his touch, and her blood began to burn for a different reason at his intense look. She ducked her head and hugged him back, breathing in his scent deeply. She even loved that about him! How was it possible to find such a perfect person?

"Why didn't you go with me to the dance when I first asked, if you felt this?" Decker's voice held a note of sadness in it.

"Because I don't understand how Light and Dark can be together when our paths seem so different," she said. She touched the amulet at his chest. His glowed black with energy.

"You haven't been listening to those boring lectures. Light and Dark need each other," he said, humor in his voice. "I scared you?"

"I think so, yes."

"When I turn eighteen in two weeks, I become the Master of Fire and Night. I'll take the place of my mother, the Dark Mistress, and will collect the souls of those witchlings who choose Dark."

His words made her feel ill again. Summer bit her lip, studying him. The boy she felt so comfortable with, who'd helped her over and over again, would become the very person the Light warned her against. Her mouth felt dry, even as her body screamed to be closer to him.

"The ... duty has fallen upon those in my family. Generation after generation." He turned away, rubbing the back of his head. "It's a curse that befell us long ago. My brother will be the Master of Light. Our mother is the Mistress of Fire and Night now and our aunt the Light Master. When the children of the Dark Master or Mistress reach eighteen, one will become Light and the other Dark."

She couldn't speak for a moment. Decker said nothing further. She wondered again what he'd done to earn his place in the Dark but feared what the answer would be. When she found her voice, she spoke.

157

"Your mother, the Mistress of ... Dark married someone from the Light. So we can be together, even if we are not the same." Her words sounded clunky.

"We belong together. At least, I *feel* we belong together. But Summer, I can't ask you to be with me if you're afraid or if what I am will drive you away." The note of anguish in his voice told her as much as his touch did.

"I want to be with you, Decker," she said. "I can't promise not to be afraid, because I still don't understand all of this. But I can promise you I feel what's between us, and I want that more than anything in my life. I've never been as happy as I am when we're dancing. You feel like my home. I've never had a home." The emotional words were out before she could stop them, like the tears that sprang up in her eyes.

Decker faced her, worried. He took her in his arms again and squeezed her against him. Summer drew deep breaths, wishing she'd been able to contain her emotions better. His magick filled her, calmed her. She wiped her face and pressed her cheek to his chest, content.

"You want to see something cool?" he asked.

"Yes!"

He took her hand and led her off the road, into the forest, along a narrow deer path. Summer thought of his words and his parents. She could be with him and not lose her soul, if his father could be with his soul-collecting mother. The revelation that Light and Dark could live in harmony relieved the remaining worry she had.

Except the part about him collecting souls. And what he'd done to be exiled to the Dark. She pushed those thoughts from her mind, not wanting to deal with anything that shadowed her newfound joy.

Decker followed the trail for a good fifteen minutes before it ended suddenly at a ravine. Before they reached the cliff, he stepped into the surrounding forest. Summer followed, grimacing as thorns caught the skin of her foot. She'd worn sandals today, and shrubs battered her feet as she made her way through the forest.

A large, flat rock rose from the forest, and Decker stepped onto it. He offered his hand again and they walked to the top of the sloping rock. When they reached the top, she gasped.

The rock jutted partially out over the valley, a wide swath of pine trees broken up by a narrow river below. The other wall of the ravine was half a mile away, a rocky wall capped with more trees.

"It's beautiful!" she exclaimed.

"At night, it looks like the moon rises and sets out of the valley," Decker said quietly. "This is called Miner's Drop."

She inched closer to the edge of the rock, stunned by the raw beauty of the new world. Decker wrapped his arms around her, and she leaned back, her head resting against his chest. The trees and cerulean sky became backdrops to the heat and magick between them. She closed her eyes, safe and content.

"I'll bring you up here one night," he said, his voice lower, huskier.

Biji's obsession with sex came back to her, and Summer was grateful he couldn't see her blushing. Being in his arms was magickal. Being in his arms without clothes? It would be pure bliss!

"Can I kiss you?" he asked.

"You don't have to ask," she said, turning in his arms. "That's what people do when they date, isn't it?"

159

"You're so sweet. I don't want to mess this up," he said.

Summer rose to her tiptoes and kissed him lightly on the lips in response. Decker's arms tightened around her, and his kiss grew deep, hungry. Summer opened her mouth timidly when he flicked his tongue between her lips.

He even *tasted* like heaven! She relaxed and let the magick and fire pulse through her with each of his kisses. Her own magick rose within her, even if it wasn't yet able to free itself. She sensed it would soon; its response to him was primal, uncontrollable.

Decker pulled away finally.

"Wow," she whispered.

"Yeah," he said just as quietly. "This could get intense quick."

She rested against him, listening to the sounds of the forest and their uneven breathing. Each kiss made her want more, while each touch made her feel more and more a part of him. He smoothed her hair with one hand.

"I don't ever want this to end," she breathed.

"Me neither."

They stayed on the rock for hours, talking and kissing, laughing and cuddling. Only when it was time for dinner did Decker lead her out of the forest towards the house. The table was already filled when they slipped in for dinner, and there were no two seats next to each other. Summer went to sit by Biji while Decker took up a seat on the other end next to his brother. Summer's whole body brimmed with happiness after her day. Despite being ravenous, she barely tasted her meal.

Afterwards, Decker walked her to her room and kissed her goodnight. He was replaced in her doorway by Biji, who looked stunned by the exchange. Summer grinned.

"Wow, really?" Biji asked, closing the door behind her. "Have you done it yet?"

"No, Biji!" Summer laughed. She twirled in the middle of her room, overwhelmed with her day.

"I had to take Tarzan out while you were making out with my man," Biji said with faux anger.

"Oh, I'm so sorry, Biji. I was just ... I don't know where the time went."

"If you were with him, it was worth it. But I noticed Tarzan didn't want to eat. Is he okay?"

Summer turned to her fawn and sat on the bed beside it. He looked calm and quiet, as usual. She checked his leg then retrieved the bottle from the dresser.

"Is this the same milk from this morning? It's probably too old," she said, opening it to sniff.

The scent made her gag. It wasn't rotten milk; someone had put something else in the bottle.

"What is this?" she asked, holding it away.

Biji took it and sniffed, making a face. "It's a spell."

"What do you mean?"

"I mean, this is probably poison."

Summer stared at her, stunned.

"I bet it was that bitch Dawn. My friend Ana said Beck threatened to leave her over what she did to you."

Crossing to her fawn, Summer wrapped her arms around it and studied it more closely, looking for signs of illness. Its long tongue flickered out against her arm and its ears twitched.

"But why hurt Tarzan?" Summer asked, distressed. "He's just a baby."

161

"Some people try to hurt things you love to get to you," Biji said, a shadow crossing her face. "I'll go get him some milk."

Summer nuzzled the soft fur on Tarzan's neck, disturbed that someone would try to poison such a sweet, defenseless creature. She'd thought Dawn mean, but to kill something was beyond mean. Tarzan was her first friend here, and she wasn't going to let anything happen to him!

Biji returned a few minutes later with fresh milk. The bottle still dripped water from where she'd washed it. Summer shifted away from Tarzan and took the bottle. He accepted it without question.

"I can't believe it," Summer murmured again, stroking the fawn's body.

"I can't believe you and Decker," Biji said. She sat on the bed across from Summer and folded her legs beneath her. "Tell me!"

"There's nothing to tell. After last night at the dance, I talked to him. And we just kinda decided we liked each other."

"Boring!" Biji said. "I can't believe that video or how Dawn tried to humiliate you. Even Beck was a jerk."

"You didn't watch the video, did you?" Summer asked, looking at her friend.

"Well ..." Biji rolled her eyes. "No, of course not. Wait, did you find the camera?"

"I gave it to Amber already," Summer said. "You really think Dawn would try to hurt Tarzan?"

"I don't know. But I can't think of anyone else who would."

"My poor Tarzan."

"When you're out with you-know-who, I'll watch him for you."

"Maybe I can take him with me, too," Summer said, considering. "I mean, if we stay around here, I can do that."

"That's a great idea. Then I can deer-sit when you're gone. But you're avoiding the subject, Summer!" Biji exclaimed. "Tell me all about him!"

Summer's troubled thoughts slid away as she told Biji about Decker. They talked long into the evening, until both were too tired to talk more. For the first time since arriving, Summer locked the door to her room, just in case someone tried to do something to Tarzan while she slept.

Chapter Eleven

THE NEXT FEW days passed as if they were a dream. Summer spent every moment she could with Decker, even sneaking kisses between classes and touching each other briefly in the halls as they passed. She kept Tarzan close to her. When Biji wasn't available to watch the fawn, Summer took him to her classes.

A week after the dance, she rested with Decker on a blanket on the rock overlooking the valley. Her gaze was on the full moon above. Just as Decker said, it had seemed to rise out of the valley and lingered over the edges of Miner's Drop, huge and bright. They lay on their sides, her body pressed against his. The fawn dozed on a pillow Summer brought for him.

"I thought you'd like it," Decker said softly.

Summer snuggled closer to him. "It's beautiful. I didn't think you wanted me in the forest after dark, though."

"If you're with me, it's okay."

She rolled onto her back, gazing up at Decker. His face was a mix of light and shadows in the bright moonlight. He kissed her tenderly, running his fingers down her face and neck, pausing at her amulets. The one containing her soul glowed faintly while the protection amulet was dark.

"I'm glad Sam gave this to you," he said. He rested his hand on her stomach. Everywhere he touched her, fire lit up her blood. Sometimes, she could barely breathe, she was so warm.

"Do you know why he did?" she asked.

"Not exactly. Some secrets I don't get to learn for another week," he said. "But if Sam thought you were in danger, I'm happy he's protecting you."

"A week," she murmured. "My birthday is the day after yours. I still can't use my magick."

Decker released more of his own into her, tickling her. She giggled in response.

"You have to find the key," he said.

She met his gaze. "I might know what it is."

Even touching, the tension between them grew thicker. Her body burned for him in a way she'd never wanted anyone else. She didn't understand the changes her body went under when he was around, but they only happened for him. She guessed he was also the only one who could sate them. Decker stroked her cheek, holding her gaze.

"Would you, um, stay with me this weekend?" he whispered. "Overnight. My family has a cabin near here. We can go there tomorrow for the weekend."

Summer's breath caught and her blood pounded in her ears. Her body screamed for her to agree, while she wondered if he'd hate her once he saw her naked. The taunts of Dawn and her friends had only gotten worse the past week.

"Yes," she managed. "Yes, Decker, I will."

He kissed her again, and she clung to him, almost sighing when his body met the length of hers. Her magick was at a shout, her need twice as loud. Something hard and long pressed against her thigh, and she shifted away.

"Sorry," he said, leaning back. "That's ..." Even in the night, he turned red.

It took Summer a minute to register why he was embarrassed. She laughed.

"You have that effect on me," he said sheepishly. "I've been trying to hide it."

"I do that to you?" she asked, grinning. She reached up to touch his face. His jaw line was rough from not shaving for a couple of days. The shading of his stubble gave him a more rugged, dangerous appearance.

"Yeah."

"Wow." She cuddled against him again, beaming with the knowledge she had such an effect on such an incredible guy.

Out of respect for him, Summer didn't mention to Biji later how turned on he was when she told her friend about the invite to the cabin. Biji's jaw dropped.

"Summer, you know what this means?" she exclaimed.

"Pretty sure I do," Summer said, laughing. "It means I beat you to it, right?"

Biji grinned. "You have to shave your legs. Don't forget that. I'll stay in your room this weekend with Tarzan. So, are you going to let him undress you or just rip off your clothes?"

Summer contemplated the question. They'd gotten hot and heavy before, and it'd been awkward to maneuver her clothing. Even the bent fasteners of her old bra got stuck whenever she tried to remove it.

"What if you try to take off your pants and trip?" Biji asked, pensive.

"That'd be awful."

"Where are your clothes?"

Summer rolled off her bed and crossed to the closet, throwing it open. She'd kept it closed since the camera incident, just in case. She didn't have much clothing and frowned at her choices.

"This is pretty." Biji pulled out a worn jean skirt. "I think you should wear a skirt, so you don't trip."

"Good idea," Summer agreed and laid it out on the bed. "If I wear a tank, I don't have to worry about unfastening a bra."

"Ooooh, yeah, I agree."

"So that's taken care of. Should I bring a shirt to sleep in?"

"Everyone knows you sleep naked. I wouldn't bother."

"Biji!" Summer murmured. "I stopped doing that because of the video. I don't even get dressed in my room anymore. I go in the bathroom."

"Naked is sexier," Biji advised. "Do you have condoms?"

"No. I figured he'd have some."

"Be back in a minute."

Summer watched her go and looked at Tarzan. The fawn was still limping, two weeks after its attack, and he hadn't grown much at all. She worried about him. As soon as her

167

stipend kicked in, she'd find a way to take him to the vet. He chewed on the sweatshirt she left on the bed. She pried it out of his mouth.

"I've got all kinds of stuff for you," Biji said, returning with her bag. She kicked the door closed behind her and dumped it. She lifted a blue square. "Condom."

"Why do you have these?" Summer asked, amused.

"You never know. I buy them at a discount online and sell them for profit to people like Dawn."

"So she and Beck are doing it?"

"Like every night, according to Ana."

"I heard the first time hurts," Summer said, sitting to sift through Biji's belongings.

"I heard that, too. You have to tell me how much. Take mouthwash, too. And this."

Summer took the travel bag of hairspray, scrunchies, and butterfly hair barrettes from her. Biji piled four condoms on top of the travel bag, a pink bottle of perfume, make-up removal pads, and an eye shadow compact with six earthy colors.

"That should get you through the weekend," Biji said, looking over the pile. She returned the rest of her belongings into her bag.

Summer fingered the delicate perfume bottle. Biji's belongings were lightly used but always looked new and expensive. Summer had nothing nearly as new or nice as her friend's.

"Thank you, Biji," she said. "I really wish I wasn't such a loser. I mean, people have to help me with everything."

"Whatever. We're friends. You let me play with your Tarzan. He's more valuable than all the stuff in my bag. Now, let's pick what you'll wear Sunday."

They returned to her closet and debated over her Sunday outfit before choosing jeans and another tank.

"I think I'll take off all my clothes before we lay down," Summer said. "I mean, that way, nothing bad happens."

"I think that's best," Biji agreed. "The skirt and tank will make it easier but you want this to be perfect. I mean, it's your first time, and with Decker." His name came out a half-sigh.

"I know." Summer chewed her lip. "I do want it to be perfect. He's so—"

"Handsome and tall and strong and perfect."

"Exactly."

Biji giggled, and Summer smiled again.

"You're sure you'll be okay alone with Tarzan?" she asked, glancing at her ward.

"Yep. I know what to feed him and not to leave him alone. We'll have fun. I'll take him in the yard and bring him berries."

"Thank you so much, Biji!" Summer hugged her.

"You're my friend. It's what friends do."

"I've gotta pack!" Summer exclaimed. "I don't want to forget anything, like a toothbrush."

"Blech!"

Summer went to the bathroom and packed her small travel bag. Biji cooed to Tarzan in the bedroom. Closing her medicine cabinet, Summer stopped to look at herself. She rarely paid attention, and most mornings, the fog from the shower kept her from seeing herself clearly.

Her dark eyes sparkled. She couldn't stop smiling, and the upturn of her lips made her face glow. Her cheeks were pink.

She'd never seen herself happy before. This place—and Decker, Tarzan, Biji—had changed her life in just over two weeks. She looked as cute as Biji claimed she was.

Her newfound confidence lasted through the night, and she met Decker in the dining area for breakfast the next morning. Afterwards, she kissed Tarzan goodbye and hugged Biji then gathered her backpack and joined Decker in the shuttle that ran to the beach on the weekends. Nervous, excited, Summer sat as close to him as possible, calmed by the magick that flowed into her. He squeezed her thigh with a small smile. They were quiet during the short ride to the beach drop-off point.

Summer climbed out ahead of him, waiting. The midmorning was warm and bright. More than a few of the teens from the school were lying in bikinis on the beach, tanning. Decker took her hand and led her in the direction opposite of the resort, around the south side of the lake. They ambled down a dirt road lined with trees.

Summer closed her eyes and breathed in the scent of pine and sunshine. The air tickled the back of her neck, and even the trees seemed to crowd her.

"They want to talk to you," Decker said.

Opening her eyes, she gasped at the sight of branches reaching for her. They couldn't quite stretch across the road and retreated, hovering protectively over her.

"Can you hear them yet?" he asked.

"No. I can't hear the air, either, but it likes to mess with me."

"The elements love those who can talk to them. The earth senses you're close to accessing your magick."

She looked up at him, grinning. He kissed her forehead.

"You think tonight ... will work?" she asked. "You really think it's the key?"

"It might be. It's different for everyone. I crashed my motorcycle last year and nearly died. Ran straight into a cliff. When I woke up a few days later, I could access my magick."

"What an awful way to unlock it."

"I hope I'm the key. It'd be the first time I was special for a reason other than to become the Dark Master."

"Can I ask how you became Dark?" When he hesitated, she rushed on. "You don't have to, if it bothers you."

"I broke one of the most sacred rules of the Light. I went beyond harming someone and killed her."

"Why?" Stunned, Summer stared up at him. Stormy emotions crossed his features. She wanted his pain to leave, so they could be happy once again, but she couldn't walk away when he'd admitted to murder.

"She asked me to."

"Will you tell me what happened?" she asked. "Please?"

Decker sighed. "She was a cancer patient who was expected to die any day. I met her when I got in my motorcycle wreck last year. She said she was in pain and wanted to die. I used my magick to help her overdose on pain meds. That's it."

"The Light condemned you for it," she mused.

"I was destined to become the Dark Master, anyway. Something would've happened to pull me off the path of the Light."

"You really think so? You don't think Beck could've been the Dark Master?"

"Beck doesn't think badly of anyone. He has no spine, which is why he puts up with Dawn. She's pulled so much

crap, she should be wearing black. He'll never be able to k …
he'll never be able to hurt anyone."

"I can see that," Summer murmured. "I think she tried
to kill Tarzan."

He stopped and turned to her. "Are you serious?"

"I don't know for sure. Someone put poison in his bottle.
He was too smart to drink it, though."

"When I turn eighteen in a week, she'll be the first one I
claim."

"She didn't kill him, though," Summer said. "I left Biji
with him to make sure nothing happens."

"Smart. It'd make it easier for me to claim her if she did
it, but not your Tarzan. I know how much you love him."

"I do," she said. "He's such a precious little guy. Biji will
take care of him."

The tension eased from Decker's frame, and they started
walking again.

"I've never really had friends, and now I have three," she
continued. "I feel like I've been given a second chance at life.
Ever feel that way?"

"Eh, not so much. My one mistake made me the Master
of Darkness," he joked. "I'd do it again, if give the chance. I
think the only thing that can save me is you."

"Really?"

"I've been headed down a dark path for a while. When
we're together, I don't feel the demons inside me."

Summer glanced up at him, hearing the pain in his voice
again. She was afraid to ask if these demons were real or just
an expression.

"I think we were made for each other," she said.
"Sometimes, that scares me."

"Me, too, usually when you're not around. I wonder how we can have something so perfect when there's nothing perfect about the world around us."

"I love it, whatever it is."

"Good. I've got another two years here and you have three. It gives us tons of us-time."

"I like the sound of that."

They walked in happy silence. Summer watched the trees they passed continue to try to reach her. Finally, she stepped away from Decker and reached out to one. It lowered its branches to her, touching her hand lightly. The long, loose pine needles felt almost like fur. She laughed at the magick tingle that went through her. Content, the tree returned to its upright position, and she retreated to Decker's side.

"Sam says you'll be very strong," Decker said. "He said you'd alter the balance."

"I'm not sure that's a good thing, is it?"

"I have no idea. But I agree that you've got a lot of potential. I felt you the day we met in the driveway."

"Amber says I'll be officially a member of the Light in a week. I hope I can help others like me out there. I think that would make everything I've been through a little less awful. Maybe I can find orphans with magick like me and rescue them. Though I really don't want to leave here. This place makes me feel at peace." Her gaze went to the trees again.

"We have to travel the world, too," he said. "We can go anywhere you want."

Summer said nothing, dazzled by the idea of spending not just a few years with him, but the rest of her life. She'd never thought beyond the next week or two. A future wasn't something she'd ever thought she'd have.

"Ireland," she said at last. "And maybe … Greece? No, southern France."

"We can go to all three," he said, chuckling. "I want to go to Machu Picchu. I saw a show on TV that said the aliens built the city in the mountains. I want to hunt for them."

"For aliens?" she asked.

"Yeah. I've been watching space shows, since you like stars."

Summer laughed.

"You never know. We exist; they might, too." He grinned.

"True!"

They talked and laughed the rest of the way to the cabin, the darkness of his past lost. When they turned down a driveway and walked around a curve, Summer almost stopped. What he called a *cabin* was a log mansion almost the size of the resort. The garage door was open, as if expecting them, and the chimney puffed smoke despite the warm day.

"This is your parents' place?" she managed as they reached the garage.

"Yep. They're in London. Beck and I come here on weekends sometimes, so they keep the staff working part time."

Staff. London. Adam had said the Turner twins' parents were well off, but she never imagined they could afford a household staff or a cabin this size.

Decker typed a code into a panel on the wall, and the door closed. He led her through a door into a stainless steel kitchen with ceilings twenty feet tall and counters stretching twenty feet. It smelled clean beneath undertones of fresh bread. To her right was a wall of windows overlooking the lake.

"Wow," she said, gazing at the lake.

"My ... our room has the same view. We're directly above the kitchen. It smells so good in the morning, when the chef makes bread."

Our room. Each moment with him grew better than the last. Decker gave her a tour of the downstairs: the two-story formal dining and living rooms, the cozier family room, game room, media room and two restrooms. They ascended to the second floor, and he showed her the upstairs living area and pool room and motioned to the doors of the master suite, Beck's room, and several guest bedrooms before opening the door to his room.

Summer stepped into his room, attention caught first at the wall of windows opposite her. His room was spacious, with a king-sized sleigh bed and heavy furniture in dark woods. Like the rest of the house, the walls were thick, caramel-colored logs. The rug underfoot dark blue. It smelled of him, a comforting scent that made her smile.

"Bathroom here," he said and opened a door opposite the windows. "The other door is a closet and behind here"— he pushed open a bi-fold screen on the wall on the other side of the bed —"a fireplace."

"This is amazing, Decker," she said, gazing around. "This is nicer than an apartment."

"It's quiet. The bed is so much better than those at the dorms." He flung himself across the bed and rolled onto his back.

Summer sat on the plush bed.

"Stars in our hemisphere. I put it up after the night we lay on the picnic table."

She looked where he pointed at the ceiling directly overhead. She lay down beside him, gazing at the round posters depicting constellations. He took her hand as they lay quietly.

"Wanna watch a movie?" he asked.

"Sure."

Hand-in-hand, they walked to the media room. Summer sank into one of the plush leather chairs and watched Decker fiddle with a remote that turned on the huge, flat-screen television. She looked around, wondering what it was like to live in such a huge house. She could see herself with Decker, ten years down the road, watching movies and talking. The vision made her smile. After twelve years in the state system, the idea of a home and a life left her awed and yearning.

They watched movies until it was dark. Decker excused himself, and she finished the last movie on her own. As the credits rolled, Summer stirred and looked around. She left the media room to find a thin trail of rose petals leading her towards the stairs and up. They continued down the hall and stopped at the door to his room.

"Decker?" she called.

Light glowed from his room. She approached, not wanting to disturb him, and paused in the doorway. The fire in the fireplace was lit, and the room smelled of earthy incense. A clear bottle sat in a wine bucket beside the fire with two delicate crystal glasses beside it. Summer's heart beat harder and harder with each step she took. Her hands shook in anticipation and excitement.

"I ran out of roses," Decker said, emerging from the bathroom. He flicked off the light, leaving them with the glow of fire that reflected in the dark windows. "I, uh, wanted it to be perfect but didn't think I needed so many. It's not wine, either. I forgot to ask the housekeeper to leave some out. It's just imported seltzer water."

"It is perfect!" she replied.

He looked relieved and rubbed the back of his head. Summer closed the door.

They stared at each other. The space between them felt like a million miles. Decker took in her face intently. She held out her hand finally, and he took it. They stood toe-to-toe.

"I just want you to know, I feel honored to be here with you," he whispered.

"I think we saved each other, Decker," she said honestly.

He kissed her. She took his face in her hands, kissing him back. Her magick stirred when his hands found her hips. Decker stepped towards the bed. Summer backed away, breaking contact.

"Wait," she said.

"What's wrong?" he asked immediately.

She shook her head and took another step back. She'd undressed herself in her thoughts over and over, so she'd get it right when it was time. Her hands shaking, she tugged off the tank top and then her skirt and underwear. When she straightened, she realized she hadn't decided what to do with her hands. She crossed her arms then dropped them, fidgeting.

Decker was silent. She looked up at long last. He was staring at her, his mouth open.

"Should I not have done that?" she asked, exposed and all too aware most of the kids at school thought she needed to lose weight.

His voice was hoarse. "My god, Summer, you're beautiful."

The flush that spread through her originated from her toes and made it all the way to the top of her head.

"You can come closer," she said when he hesitated.

Decker's gaze took in her naked body, lingering on her breasts then traveling down to the apex of her thighs. He did as she beckoned, rubbed the back of his head, and touched her gently. His hand shook as bad as hers as it traveled down her shoulder and arm before tentatively findings its place on her hip.

"You're so soft," he whispered, awed. "Like the rose petals."

Summer's breathing was uneven. His touch burned her bare skin, his agitated magick flying through her with the same urgency she felt. Carefully, Decker touched her with his other hand. His large hands were gentle enough to tickle, as if he feared her skin would tear as easily as a rose petal.

Chapter Twelve

"IT'S OKAY, DECKER," she said. "You won't hurt me." She took his hands and pressed them against her hips.

He felt silly as soon as she said the words. He'd had sex before, but this was different. This was *Summer.* Firelight and shadows flickered over Summer's naked body. He didn't know what possessed her to take off her clothes all at once, but he liked it.

No, he loved it. He loved the silkiness of her skin, the feminine shape of her body, her heady scent. Dark hair was draped over one shoulder, hiding half of one plump breast. He took in her body again, from her bright eyes to the soft curls at the apex of her thighs. He hadn't even let himself dream of this moment, in case it never happened. Standing before her, he began to think this was as close to heaven as a condemned soul would ever get.

He lifted her hair to reveal both breasts and trailed a finger down her chest and stomach.

"Are you disappointed?" she ventured at his silence.

"No. Never with you." He met her gaze again.

"I know I'm overweight." Her nervous words were accompanied by a small laugh.

"You're perfect."

"You still want me, right?"

He almost laughed at the concerned look that crossed her face. As if he could walk away from her! As if she wasn't the sole reason his heart beat!

"Yes, Summer. More than anything," he said. He took one of her hands and placed it along the ridge in his pants. "See?"

She flushed then grinned. Her hand stayed when he released her, and he cupped her face in his hands.

"I'm yours, Summer. Forever and ever, if you want," he said.

"Really?"

He nodded. Her soul sang louder, happier than any he'd ever heard. The sound made him want to wrap himself in her arms forever.

"I'm yours, too, Decker. Forever and ever, if you want me."

"I do."

"Promise?"

"Yeah. With all my soul," he whispered. "I could never be with anyone else."

"I promise, too."

He leaned back and peeled off his T-shirt. Summer touched him tentatively, her fingers tickling the thin layer of hairs on his chest. She flattened her palms against his pecs, and he reveled in the sensations of her magick trickling from deep within her into his body. Her cool hands branded him everywhere they touched.

He kissed her, long and deep. His restraint began to slip, and he gathered her into his arms. She was so soft and warm, so sweet and eager. He wanted to take his time and handle her carefully, like the delicate treasure she was, but his desire was rising fast and hot. Summer was matching his hunger kiss for kiss, touch for touch.

"I need you," he said against her mouth.

"What're you waiting for?" she replied.

Decker didn't need a second invitation. He bent and lifted her, carrying her to his bed. He set her down gently and stood back, admiring once again. She reached for him, and he peeled off his jeans and boxers before lying beside her. They kissed, her hands exploring his body so lightly, they tickled him.

Their first time didn't go as he planned. He lasted less than sixty seconds, too excited after the condom went on. It was probably for the best; Summer had been uncomfortable with her first time. She went to the bathroom, and he lay still. When Summer returned to the bed, he wasn't sure what she'd say, if she wanted to leave. She crawled in beside him and lay facing him. Naked, they gazed at each other.

"Did it hurt?" he asked.

"A little," she replied. "Did it hurt you?"

"God no! It made me want to do it again and again and again." He kissed her with each *again* then fluttered kisses over her face until she laughed.

Decker pressed her to the bed again and kissed her deeply. He let his hands roam her soft skin. He was ready again. Drunk off her scent, enthralled by the shadows of her body, he didn't think he'd ever get enough of his Summer.

"Wanna try again?" he whispered.

"Yeah."

He complied, this time slower, more controlled. As he made love to her, he felt the shift within her. The trickle of her magick turned into a flood. His own power tempered the release, absorbing the newly freed magick, while he lost himself in the sensations of her body.

They made love once more. Each time grew sweeter, longer. When they'd finished, Summer curled up against him and fell asleep. Decker held her naked body close. Sated and calm, he focused on her magick.

She'd been right. He was the key to unlocking it. He brushed the hair from her face, smiling. She'd surrendered to him in a way he didn't think was possible, and he'd done for her what no one else could.

Sam said she was strong, and Decker roused himself, assessing. His shadows explored the depths of her magick. She was the exact opposite of him. Rather than repelling each other, their magickks complemented one another. When he pushed, hers gave. When hers pushed, his gave.

They were perfect partners in every way. His hand traveled down her side and rested on her hip. Was this the connection his parents felt? Was this what kept his mother from madness?

He'd never asked his parents what it'd been like when they met. But he could easily imagine Summer becoming a counterbalance to any darkness he encountered. His mind was calm and quiet with her and nothing else.

He dozed for a short time. A tingle of warning woke him. His magick was churning the way it did whenever Beck was about to hit him. Decker blinked away sleep and left the bed, covering Summer with the blankets before he pulled on his jeans and left the room.

He didn't recognize what it was his magick tried to tell him. It was there, just out of his reach, like the secrets Sam kept for after his transition. Decker stood in the middle of the hallway on the bottom floor, listening. After a long moment, he heard the muffled sound of voices. They came from outside the house.

Burglars? In Priest Lake? The village-sized town had virtually no crime, especially during summer months. Most tourists came for the winter skiing, not the relatively weak summer sun. He went to the coatroom and pulled on a sweatshirt and boots. He'd heard the sounds from the front of the house.

Decker strode through the kitchen and garage, exiting into the night. His magick unfurled protectively around him. The sense of danger grew as he moved silently through the forest towards the front of the house. When he reached a vantage point looking out onto the front of the house, he paused in the shadows. The cabin faced the lake. Moonlight reflected off the water in waves and ripples.

A form darted across the patio into the forest that sloped towards the lake. He heard the voices again, this time more clearly. He could pinpoint where they came from, even if he couldn't quite make out the words. His gaze lingered on the patio. The patio door was locked from the inside. It didn't look open or the windows along the front of the house broken. Reassured no one was in the house, Decker moved towards the sounds of the men talking.

There were three. He neared, but they were retreating towards the lake. He hesitated, his magick warning him still of a threat. Decker retreated to the patio and climbed over the railing. He heard the low sizzle a moment before fire exploded on one end of the house and flew down the logs lining the bottom of the windows.

His instincts took over. His magick surged, roaring towards the fire before it could spread. The patio flamed with brightness as he wrapped the living flames up in his magick. Feeding off their energy, Decker closed his eyes and spread his arms, letting them swirl around him before his darkness sucked them into his body, extinguishing them.

The world fell quiet and dark again. He faced the lake.

Someone tried to hurt Summer. Maybe they were after him or his family, but he began shaking at the thought Summer might've been hurt instead.

Without her near him, the black rage returned, this time agitated by fire. He vaulted over the patio railing and tore into the forest. His magick grew with his fury, and it pushed aside any branches that might block him and bushes that would trip him. Breathing hard, he reached the lake just as a small boat pushed off from the private dock. His father's fishing boat was on one side, the small dinghy on the other. The three men within were paddling to keep from using the loud motor.

Adrenaline and magick took hold. Decker dived into the cold water and swam towards the boat with powerful strokes. The water elemental's distant trickle grew to the roar of a waterfall as the magick engaged and thrust him forward even faster.

One hand smacked into the boat. Decker bobbed a moment to catch his breath before the water lifted him. Off balance, he all but fell into the boat.

"What the f—"

"Don't," Decker said, the water warning him of the gun one reached for. He stood opposite the three men in black. The man with the gun had frozen, and the other two looked equally shocked. "Just tell me why you were burning my house, and I won't hurt you."

One broke the silence with a surprised laugh. He pulled out the gun. Before he could point it, his wrist was grabbed by a tendril of water that snaked over the side of the boat. The other two men moved away, staring.

"It's a simple question," Decker said. His breathing calmed, and so did the fury within him. It focused on the three. "Why were you trying to burn down my house?"

"Look, kid, it's nothing personal. Just swim home and we'll leave you alone," one replied.

The idea they'd meant to hurt Summer without caring what they did made him snap. Decker pointed at the man with the gun. The water grabbed him and pulled him into its depths. The man barely got off a cry of surprise before he was submerged. For the first time since his mother killed a man in front of him, he understood why she had neither remorse nor pity.

"Answer the question. He's dying now, but he doesn't have to," he told them.

"What are you?"

"In about five minutes, it won't matter."

Release him, son.

He cocked his head to the side, not certain he heard his mother's voice.

Decker, now.

He ordered the water to return the man to the surface. The wave flung him into the boat at the feet of the other two men.

185

"You're not above the Laws, yet, son."

He turned at the soft voice of his mother. Decker's anger faded. She was dressed in a white ski suit, as if they'd been skiing when she decided to appear on the boat.

"Go," she said and tossed her head to the side.

"Mother, I—"

"I'll take care of it. Wait for me on the patio."

Decker stared at his mother. He wanted to object, but something in her dark gaze and even darker aura warned him against it. He stepped onto the edge of the boat and dove into the water. Surfacing a few feet away, he glanced back at his mother. She was talking to the men in her quiet, deadly tone.

He swam back to the dock and hauled himself out. He did what she said and made his way up the hill towards the patio. When he got there, she was waiting. Decker twisted to see the dinghy on fire in the middle of the lake a moment before the dark water swallowed it whole. The night was chilly, and he shivered.

"You can't kill until you're eighteen, Decker," his mother reminded him. She crossed her arms. "Killing humans is a tough line to cross."

"But you just did it."

"There were compelling reasons."

"Like trying to burn our house down?"

"No. They failed at that but weren't exactly innocent souls."

Her casual tone made him shiver again, this time in unease. He'd never feared his mother before he went to the Dark. Even after, he'd never thought her capable of what she did until he saw her do it firsthand. She'd turned from loving mother into feared mentor.

"Want to tell me what exactly happened?" she asked.

"Nothing, Mother," he said. "Thanks." He started towards the house.

"Who's the girl in your bed?"

He froze in midstride, his chest seizing at the thought his mother could do something—anything—she wanted to Summer. It took him a moment before he could breathe again. Summer had done nothing wrong; his mother couldn't touch an innocent soul.

"I can play hardball, too, son."

"I woke up in the middle of the night. I don't know why, but my magick was disturbed. I came outside and saw the three guys. There's lighter fluid or gasoline or something all over the back of the house," he said and looked up, smelling it. "The fire started. I put it out and chased them down."

His mother turned to look at the house. The bases of the logs looked black in the moonlight.

"It wasn't an accident," he added. "Did they say who they were or why they did this?"

"They were hired by an anonymous woman who paid cash."

Decker's thoughts went to Alexa then Dawn. Either of them could've done this, though it seemed far-fetched. Alexa had sworn vengeance, but she came from a poor family. She wouldn't have the cash to pay anyone. Dawn's family, on the other hand, was well off. He didn't see any reason for her to do this, though. She had Beck, and she'd humiliated Summer at the dance.

"You know who it was?" she asked.

"No, I don't," he replied, puzzled.

"You suspect someone?"

"A couple of people, but it doesn't make sense." His gaze went upwards, towards his room, where Summer slept.

"And the girl?" his mother prodded.

"What does it look like, Mother?" he returned.

"It looks like my son is hiding something from me."

"So I brought a girl home. Beck does it all the time."

"Maybe. But you don't."

"I don't want to talk about it," he said.

"Very well, Decker." Her voice softened. "I'm worried about you."

"I'll be fine."

"I wasn't."

"I just … I just want to go inside." *Back to Summer,* he added silently.

His mother made no response. Decker walked away. He'd wanted to ask her about his father and when they met. He couldn't find the words. All he could think about was silencing the noise in his head. He half-expected his mother to follow him. She didn't, and he returned to his room. He showered to get the lake smell off him then slid into bed beside Summer, grateful she still slept.

Chapter Thirteen

SUMMER AWOKE TO the scents of burnt cinnamon and bacon. She rolled over, not recognizing where she was for a moment. The passionate night returned to her, and she sighed. Her whole body still hummed like it did when Decker touched her, even if he wasn't in the bed. She rose and dressed in his T-shirt, loving his scent on it.

She followed the rose petals towards the stairs and down, finding her way to the kitchen. Decker had made a mess of the kitchen in his quest to make the burnt French toast and crispy bacon sitting on a plate on the counter. Summer sat at the breakfast bar and watched him, smiling. The tenderness and sensitivity he'd shone in bed was nowhere in sight as he tried to juggle a toaster, frying pan, and microwave.

When he dropped French toast on the floor with a curse, she laughed. He turned, startled.

"Hey," he said, a smile drawing across his face.

"Hey."

Both blushed at the long look, and he returned to the stove. Summer approached him and wrapped her arms around him. He turned and hugged her.

"I ruined breakfast," he said. "I hope you like cereal."

"I love it!" she said, chuckling.

He nuzzled her hair and sighed. "How do you feel?"

"A little sore," she admitted.

"Me, too. I wasn't expecting that. Your magick?"

Her magick. She'd been too lost in happiness to notice. Summer stepped away until she broke contact with him.

It was free. It moved through her as Decker's had.

"I think it worked," she said.

"I was hoping it hadn't so we could try again."

She grinned. "We can."

"Sounds like we have a date tonight."

She wanted to scream out of joy but twirled in the middle of his kitchen instead. She was sore, but the happiness and magick within her drowned out the discomfort of her first time. The air swirled around her, lifting her hair up. It hugged her and pulled her off the floor a foot.

Summer yelped and reached for Decker. He laughed and took her hand, pulling her back down.

"You'll have to learn to talk to them, soon, or they'll drive you crazy," he advised. "I can show you some things today."

True to his word, they went to the patio after breakfast and showers. On the patio were two circles with pentagrams in their centers. One circle was black on white stone, the other white on black stone.

"This is my mother's and mine," Decker said, motioning to the black circle. "That one is for Father and Beck. You can use it. This point is north." He indicated the arm of the pentagram pointing towards the lake.

Summer stepped into the center of the pentagram. Nothing happened. She looked around. Decker was pulling candles out of a stone trunk that doubled as a bench lining the other side of the patio. He placed one at each point of both pentagrams then lit them. The scent of the candles was pungent, like a room full of herbs.

"The first few times will be hard," he said, standing outside her circle. "You can sit down or lie down or stand. You want to be relaxed, until you can learn to mold the magick."

Summer sat cross-legged, facing the lake.

Decker sat outside the circle. "Okay, now close your eyes and take five deep breaths."

She obeyed, filling her lungs with the earthy scents. Her body began to relax.

"The first thing you have to learn is how to find your magick. Then you can focus it."

The churning power within her felt both like it was within her grasp and slipping through her fingers. It seemed more interested in exploring her body. She concentrated hard on finding out where it hid inside her. It seemed to be densest in her upper abdomen.

"I think I found it," she said. "But it's like trying to grab fog."

"Relax. If you're tense, it'll push back. Remember, it's a part of you."

She didn't tell him it wasn't natural to have magick swimming in her body. Sam had compared it to a wild creature, one that seemed more interested in its own actions than hers.

"Deep breaths," Decker urged. "The pentagram helps you focus your elements, but you have to focus the internal magick."

She drew another deep breath and felt her shoulders relax. The magick didn't seem to want to be focused. She tried for several more minutes.

"It's being stubborn," Decker said, thoughtful. "Focus outwards instead on the air and earth."

She felt a difference instantly as she became more aware of her surroundings. The air sounded as if it was laughing, the sound like the distant tinkling of wind chimes. It didn't speak words she could understand, but it chattered around her and flicked her hair. The stone beneath her grew warm.

"Good," Decker whispered. "Pull them to you."

Summer focused on the wind first and hearing the laughter. It grew louder, the wind stronger around her until it formed a little cyclone around the circle. She opened her eyes, surprised to *see* the wind, like glitter caught in glue. It circled her with its cheerful chatter, whipping her clothes and hair. Grinning, Decker had moved away to give it room.

"Close your eyes again and focus on your magick."

She stared at the glittery wind for a moment longer then closed her eyes. The magick had stopped roaming her body and pooled in her abdomen. She tried to push it mentally, but it didn't budge. Just sat, as if mesmerized by the wind like she had been.

"No, no," Decker called over the tinkling sounds. "Don't *push* the magick. Pull it."

Perplexed, Summer did nothing for a moment, not at all certain how to pull something out of her that didn't want to come. She couldn't even grab it and try.

"It's okay," Decker said at last. "We'll try it again later. Can you send the wind away?"

Summer focused outwards again and imagined herself pushing the wind away. The sounds and sensations faded until she heard only the distant tinkling again.

"You did awesome," Decker said when she opened her eyes.

"I didn't do it, though," she said, disappointed.

"It takes awhile. I promise, by the time we leave here, you'll be able to do it."

"Did you hear the sounds the wind made?"

"No. Only you can. You'll hear it everywhere you go. You can call it to you whenever you want. Did the earth respond, too?"

"The stone got hot," she said, placing her hand on the stone. "But it didn't make any sounds."

"It will. Your dominant element is talking to you. The secondary will follow."

"You have three elements?"

"Yeah. It's like noise in my head at all times."

"What do they sound like?" she asked.

"Fire sounds like the crackling of a bonfire and water like a creek. Spirit ..." He grew pensive. "It changes. Sometimes, it's like laughter and sometimes, it's like someone crying. When I met you, it cried. But now, it laughs. Sam says Spirit reads the souls of those around me."

"That's incredible."

"It's overwhelming. I go insane being in a crowd. The mandatory dinners are painful for me. I get headaches almost every day."

She frowned at the look of pain that crossed his face. The tinkling in the back of her mind was cheerful and light. She couldn't imagine the bombardment Decker went through if each person he crossed gave off a sound.

"I'm so sorry, Decker," she said.

"It's okay. My burden," he said with a tight smile. "We're a complete set of elements."

"A perfect match."

"Agreed." He held out his hand and pulled her up. "We'll take a break and try again a little later."

They spent the rest of the day alternately testing her ability and relaxing in the media or game rooms. By sunset, she heard the tinkling of air and distant hum of the earth, like the low grumble of a bass guitar. Even so, the magick within her resisted her attempts to focus it. When she was tired of trying, Decker pulled her to her feet, and they retreated for a dinner prepared by the house chef, who left with a smile as they sat down to eat.

She gazed at Decker over dinner, noticing the shadow that crossed his features more than once. Touching his foot with hers under the table, she smiled when he looked at her, and the darkness receded. After dinner, they walked hand-in-hand to the media room to watch another movie.

As they sat down, the door between the kitchen and garage slammed closed. Decker sprang to his feet, his magick rippling in the air around them. He was halfway to the door of the media room when Beck's voice rang out.

"Hey, guys! Where you at?"

194

Decker relaxed visibly, and Summer gazed at him with a frown. He'd reacted as if threatened, like someone was trying to break in.

"Media room!" he answered and flipped on the overhead lights.

Beck entered a few minutes later, his dark hair tousled. He smiled at Summer, not at all surprised she was there. She fidgeted, wondering if he thought poorly of her still after the dance.

"Is your eye black?" Decker asked, peering closely at his twin.

"Probably."

"Any reason why?"

"Eh, girl troubles."

Decker grew tense again. Summer gazed at him, sensing something amiss without knowing what.

"No worries," Beck said with a grin at her. "Roll the movie, Decker! Hope we're not watching a chick flick." He sat down beside her.

Decker hesitated, appearing to debate silently before he finally turned off the lights. He pushed Beck out of his seat and reclaimed it, settling beside her. Summer took his hand, satisfied as their magickks mixed. Decker's body relaxed the moment he touched hers, the strange tension forgotten.

Beck entertained them through half the movie, making her laugh with his off-the-cuff remarks to the dialogue on the screen. Decker smiled as well. His head rested against the back of the chair as he watched through half-closed eyes. His hand stayed on her thigh in a relaxed display of possession. Her body had been filled with fluttering and heat all day; she couldn't wait to feel his skin against hers again.

195

The flick ended, and Beck turned on the lights. Summer cuddled closer to Decker, who kissed her forehead and nipped at her ear lobe.

"Before things get awkward for me," Beck said, mimicking Decker as he rubbed the back of his head. "Summer, I owe you an apology."

She looked up at him curiously.

"For the dance thing, the letters, the video, and the curses. The list gets longer every time I stop to think about it," he joked.

"What do you mean?" she asked, face warm at the reminder of the video. "You already apologized for the dance and you had nothing to do with the video and letters. I don't know anything about curses."

"Yeah, well." Beck looked at Decker. The two exchanged a silent communication.

Summer looked between them, not understanding.

"There's been some weird stuff going on," Beck said at last. "I'll let Decker explain. I'm turning in for the night."

"Wait, Beck." Decker rose. "I talked to Mother last night. I have to show you something."

Summer watched them leave together, talking quietly. Feeling left out, she remained in the comfortable seat for a few minutes then left, padding down the hallway towards the kitchen. She paused at the island in the center and leaned against it.

The twins stood outside on the patio, talking. Their demeanors were grave. Beck's arms were crossed as he listened to what looked like a bad tale from Decker, who appeared agitated. Summer resisted the urge to comfort him. Whatever business they had, it was between them. She nibbled on cookies the chef left out.

The two spoke for another ten minutes before returning to the kitchen. Beck forced a smile while Decker reached for her. Summer felt him relax when they touched. He circled her and wrapped his arms around her, resting his chin on the top of her head.

Beck's smile grew more genuine as he studied them.

"Perfect," he said. "You take care of my brother, Summer. I know he'll take care of you."

"I will," she said, grinning.

"Just make sure you're up for the shuttle," he told Decker. "Unless you found where the parents hid our birthday presents."

"Nope."

"I had no idea they could make a car disappear." Beck shook his head, winked, and walked down the hallway.

"Your parents got you a car?" she asked.

"They got him a car. I got a motorcycle."

"Wow. I can ride with you?"

"Of course."

The thought of rugged Decker on a motorcycle with an unshaven jaw made her lower belly heat with desire.

"Okay, I want to tell you what Beck was talking about," Decker said grudgingly. He shifted away and took her hand, leading her to the small breakfast nook.

Summer sat. He pulled a chair closer to her and took her hands.

"Basically, Dawn's been putting curses on you since you got here," he said. "I think that's why Sam gave you the amulet. Well that or ..." His features grew dark again. He shook it off. "Anyway, I guess she had a curse on you the first few days that made your food taste bad. Did it taste bad?"

"Like fish." Summer frowned. "She did that? Why?"

197

"Some girls are just crazy." The way he said it made her think he was talking about more than just Dawn. "I guess Amber fixed that. When Amber left you at the mall, it was because Dawn put a spell on the van to make it seem like you were there. And the letters to you were all done by one of her friends. She also wrote about twenty letters to Beck and signed your name to them."

Summer drew a sharp breath.

"The video, which, by the way, wow." Decker's eyes gleamed. "But she did those things to you."

"But why?" Summer asked again. "I've been bullied by all kinds of people, usually because of my magick. I was no threat to her."

"She's kinda like that," he said vaguely. "Beck broke up with her, which is why he has a black eye and is here tonight."

"She did that? Awful."

"The amulet will protect you. Um, Summer, I need to ask a favor and I can't really say why."

"Of course," she said instantly. "Anything."

Decker's gaze warmed. "If you're not with me, I need you to stay on the school grounds. They're protected from major spells and curses. No more trips to the forest. Stay within the Square or dorms or classes."

"You think something is wrong?"

"I think you're a good target for Dawn and ... others who might want to get back at Beck or me. Neither of us can do anything about it until we're eighteen. You're safe with me and at the school." The darkness crossed his features again.

"I trust you, Decker," she said. "You'll be eighteen soon, anyway. Like, in a day."

"And you'll be seventeen in two," he said, smiling. "We'll have to celebrate."

She flushed at his intense look, delighted he wanted her the way he did.

"We should start now," he decided and rose, pulling her up with him. "I have a couple of ideas."

Summer laughed and wrapped her arms around him. She never imagined she'd be happy anywhere, let alone in a boarding school in the Rockies. Being with Decker was the most natural thing in the world, and she could see them together for a long, long time.

He led her up the stairs and to his room, where the fire burned. Instead of stripping for him, she let him peel her clothing off and trail kisses all over her body.

Chapter Fourteen

DECKER WATCHED SUMMER climb the stairs to the main house. She turned when she reached the door and waved. He waved back and remained until she'd disappeared inside.

"You got it bad," Beck said from behind him.

Decker ignored him and reached down to grab his gym bag. He'd never felt as whole or as good as he did this morning, even if it was too early for his preference.

"It reminds me of that vibe between Mother and Father," Beck added.

This caught Decker's attention, and he faced his twin. He expected to see the gleam in Beck's eye indicating his twin was teasing. Beck was serious.

"You really think so?" Decker asked uncertainly.

"Yeah. I think it's a really good thing for you. No hard feelings over the dance and Dawn fiasco?"

"None."

"Okay, good." Beck appeared relieved. The twinkle appeared in his eyes. "You hold a grudge like no other and are about to have the power of god to do what you want to people."

"Never to you, though," Decker said. "We might've killed each other before ... you know."

"Nothing like a horrible family secret to bring us closer together."

Decker smiled in silent agreement. The house and dorms were quiet, with only a couple of students out jogging so early. They walked past the house and into the square between dorms. Beck slowed as they neared their room.

"I'll protect you and go first," Decker said dryly. He twisted the knob to their door and entered. Their room looked the way they'd left it. He stretched his senses for any sort of curse or danger but felt nothing. "It's fine."

Beck crossed the threshold, uneasy despite Decker's words. Decker suspected something else was going on. His twin closed and locked the door before tossing his stuff on his bed.

"What if your psycho and my psycho got together?" Beck mused. "Ever think of that? One has the money and the other is Dark. No risk."

"I don't think so," Decker replied. "Trying to burn our house down is just stupid-crazy."

"It does reek of desperation, though. You have to admit, both of them are probably capable."

"I bet our mother knows who did it."

"Probably. She's kinda good at keeping secrets, though."

201

Decker met his twin's gaze. Beck still looked uncomfortable. He looked away and replaced his clothing in his drawer.

"Two days," Decker said quietly. "Summer's birthday is the day after ours. I need to get her something. You're better at this than me. What do girls like?"

"Summer would be hard. Dawn just demanded what she wanted," Beck answered. "Clothes, shoes, jewelry, perfume. Wanna ditch and go to the mall today?"

"What's wrong with you?"

"Nothing. Just don't want to be here today."

"Then let's ditch."

Beck brightened. The good one, Beck rarely did anything that might earn him a stern look from the instructors, let alone want to skip a whole day. They'd given up trying to rein in Decker. It didn't help that he couldn't tolerate being around people and just left class at will.

"I'll meet you out front," Beck said.

Nodding, Decker sat down to change shoes as his brother left. He strode out of their room a few minutes later. Matilda had just closed the door to the kitchen when he reached the corner of the dorms. She was dressed in workout clothing, but her expression was severe. He glanced at her.

"Decker, do you have a minute?" she asked.

"I guess."

She opened the door to the kitchen and held it for him. Decker entered, at once struck by the scents of breakfast. His stomach came to life. He stopped to look over fresh breakfast pastries as Matilda strode by him. Snagging one, he bit into the warm, buttery croissant and trailed her.

Amber was in her office, perched on the corner of a desk. She looked equally as worried. Both women were troubled.

202

Matilda sat in one of the chairs in front of her desk, and Decker took the other. He polished off the croissant.

"We had something happen yesterday," Matilda started. "We just want to ask you a few questions."

"Okay," he said, uncertain why they were acting so weird.

"You were at your cabin this weekend?"

"Yep."

"With Summer?"

"Yep."

"And Beck?"

"He got there last night," he said. He wondered if this had something to do with someone trying to burn down his house and leaned forward, waiting for one of them to explain what was going on. "Why?"

"It appears he and Dawn had an altercation yesterday," Amber said. "She's been beat up. She's not in the hospital or anything, but she had to go in yesterday for a broken nose."

Decker stared at her.

"We're trying to reconstruct what happened."

"And you think what?" he asked at last. "That *Beck* did this?"

"We don't know what happened," Amber said. The two instructors exchanged a look.

Anger bloomed in Decker's chest. "You know Beck would never hit anyone. He showed up to the house with a black eye, though, because Dawn doesn't have his sense of restraint."

"Until we can confirm what happened, Beck might be in some trouble," Amber said.

"Wait, did she say he hit her?"

"We're talking suspension, Decker," Matilda added.

"If Dawn said it, you know it's a lie!" he exclaimed and rose, pacing to the window. "I can't believe you, Amber. You know Beck isn't capable of doing something like this." Yes, Beck had been acting weird since last night, but he'd never hurt anyone. It wasn't him.

"Sometimes there are extenuating circumstances."

"Like what?" He faced them again, arms crossed. "What would make Beck flip out and hit his girlfriend?"

"She told him she's pregnant," Matilda said. "Her friends say he flipped out and they got into a physical altercation."

Idiot! he screamed at his brother silently. But he shook his head firmly.

"She's been after our trust funds for years. Her friends will do whatever she says," he said. "Amber, you know she's been putting curses on Summer. Before Summer, it was anyone who looked at Beck the wrong way. Her friends will do whatever she tells them to do."

"Even so, Decker, there are three girls who are supporting Dawn's story," Amber said.

Fire blazed through him. He wanted to strangle his brother for knocking up the crazy girl and Dawn for being crazy. He wanted to tell them about the woman who hired thugs to burn his house down. Instead, he fumed in silence.

"He has no other alibi but what the girls say he does," Matilda added. "We're calling your parents. For now, he'll have to stay off the school grounds on official suspension."

Beck's desire to leave—and probably avoid Dawn— made more sense, even though Decker suspected his twin had no idea what had played out since yesterday.

"It'll affect his ceremony," Amber said with a frown. "We will need to know for certain what happened before then."

Decker hadn't considered the impact to the ceremony that would change him to the Master of Fire and Night and his brother to the Master of Light. The Light ceremony took place on school grounds, but if they put up a spell to keep Beck off the property, it couldn't happen.

"So you're just going to let that lying bitch prevent the succession of the Master of Light?" he demanded. "One of the most sacred magick ceremonies?"

"We have no choice," Matilda said. "If your parents can make it back today or tomorrow, we'll be able to figure out what to do. We'll have to postpone his ceremony and Summer's."

Summer would be fine; her path was beyond any doubt. While it irked him, he didn't think she'd mind as much as Beck, who'd been prepared for this day his whole life. Fury rose within him again. He still didn't know who tried to burn the house, and now, Dawn was playing the victim.

No part of him doubted his brother. His mother could fix this; she'd know who was guilty by means of her gift for sensing evil.

"Why are you telling me this?" he asked at last, after he'd reined in his anger enough to speak in a level voice.

"If the Mistress doesn't return in time, your ceremony will still go forth," Matilda said. "It will cause an imbalance."

"There cannot be a Dark Master if there is no Light Master," Amber added.

"Easy. Go through with his ceremony," he snapped. "Deal with this crap after."

"If he did as Dawn said, the issue becomes he will no longer be on the path of Light."

Decker shook his head, ready to object again that only his mother could determine such a thing, when Matilda held up her hand.

"We have to take precautions," she said with firmness in her voice.

"You'll both be sent away," Amber said. "Temporarily."

His mind went to Summer. "It won't happen. My mother will be here soon and straighten this all out."

"I hope so. Things don't look good. Dawn's already contacted her parents and her father's attorneys. Allegedly, there's a video of what happened, and it's sitting with the attorneys right now."

Decker cursed under his breath. If that was the case, his father's attorneys had been called as well. Once attorneys got involved, there was no telling what would happen.

"I refuse to believe Beck did any of this," he said. "If he doesn't have his ceremony, I will. And when I confirm she's lied to everyone, I'll take more than her soul!"

Amber looked taken aback at his words, and Matilda sighed. Decker's mind reeled in disbelief that anyone would stand in the way of the ceremony or that all it took for them to drop it was one crazy girl's lies.

Sounds of shouting emanated from the main house. He turned. Amber was the first to the door, followed by Matilda. Furious, Decker paced for a moment before trailing to see what the commotion was about. He half hoped someone had pushed Dawn down the stairs.

"Stop this! Right now!" Amber shouted.

Decker jogged to the end of the hall and stopped, startled to see Summer and Dawn wrestling and punching. Beck had heard the sounds from outside and stood in the doorway, looking as confused as Decker felt. His twin moved first and snatched Summer off the ground, twisting until his body was between her and Dawn. Two of Dawn's friends hauled her away. Dawn started screaming insults, until Matilda clapped her hands and boomed,

"Enough! What is going on?"

Summer clutched in his arms, Beck turned slowly to look at her. Her nose and lip were bloodied. Her eyes flashed in anger.

"She attacked me!" Dawn shouted. "Crazy bitch just—

"Bullshit!" Biji shouted from the top of the stairwell. "Dawn walked in and—

"Shut up, Biji, you don't know!" one of Dawn's friends shouted.

A shouting match ensued. Summer said nothing and moved away from Beck, touching her bloodied face. She saw Decker at last and met his gaze. A look of misery and longing crossed her features, and he ached to touch her, too. He moved closer, head pounding hard at the enraged souls that screamed inside his head.

Amber and Matilda managed to silence everyone. Matilda took Dawn and her friends into the kitchen while Amber stayed in the hallway. Beck stayed where he was by the door. Summer hastened to Decker's side, taking his hand as soon as she was close enough to. His mind fell silent, but her soul was crying and her body shaking. Worried, he dabbed away the blood from her face with his T-shirt.

"Biji, *calmly* tell me what happened," Amber directed.

The small Indian girl trotted down the stairs. "We were sitting in Summer's room when Dawn almost busted down the door. She started shouting horrible things at Summer, like threatening Tarzan and stuff. Summer told her to get out and Dawn tried to grab Tarzan. Summer pushed her and then Dawn went off and punched her."

"Summer, is that what happened?" Amber asked.

"She hurt Tarzan," Summer said, clenching his hand with both of hers. "Knocked him off the bed and hurt his leg."

"She went psycho," Biji added.

"And you were there for this, Biji?" Amber asked.

"Yep. I saw the whole thing."

"Who else was there?"

"No one but us."

"I didn't see them until they fell down the stairs," Beck said.

"Okay. Biji, go help Summer clean up. We'll call the doc to drop by later today. I can't believe you fell down the stairs and aren't hurt."

Decker started to go with Summer, when Amber said his name.

"Decker, the issue we discussed earlier." Her eyes were on Beck.

Summer looked up at him questioningly. Decker looked from Biji to Beck.

"I have to go for now," he said to Summer. "I'll be back later, hopefully before my ceremony. If not, I'll come as soon as it's over, okay?"

Summer appeared disappointed but nodded. He kissed her on the forehead and released her. Decker waited until she and Biji were up the stairs before turning to Beck, who looked puzzled but not upset.

"What's going on?" Beck asked.

"We're going to the mall," Decker answered. "Call me, Amber, and tell me what happens."

Amber hesitated. At his sharp look, she nodded. Decker pushed his unsuspecting brother onto the porch.

"We gotta talk, Beck."

208

"That doesn't sound good."

"It's not." Decker climbed into the van, followed by Beck. The driver started the vehicle and drove them towards the main road leading to the lake. "Let us out once we get past the turnoff."

"Dude, what's going on?" Beck demanded. "I walk in to see Summer and Dawn falling down the stairs, and you're being all weird."

"We have to go see Sam," Decker said. "I don't have a clue what to do."

Summer finished up her shower. She dressed with hands that still shook, unsettled by both Dawn's insanity and her own actions. For the first time in her life, she'd hit someone, albeit in self-defense.

She left the bathroom to see Biji, Amber and a man in a polo seated in the room with a black bag next to him. Biji still held the fawn, who appeared to be dozing.

"I see bruises," Amber said, rising.

Summer held out her arms. Amber looked her over before stepping aside for the doctor.

"Anything hurting?" he asked.

"My elbow," she said and held out her right arm. "It's not bad though."

"No idea how you guys managed to walk away with nothing broken," Amber said.

"Youth," the doctor replied with a warm smile. He bent Summer's arm and poked at her elbow. "Probably a sprain. The swelling isn't bad. Lots of bruises, and that lip shouldn't need stitching."

209

Summer touched her lower lip. It was too swollen to smile. The doctor turned her head to look at the tender bruise on her cheek and stepped back.

"I'll give you some pain meds and antibiotic balm for the lip," he said. He turned to Amber. "The arm should be okay in a week or so. I'll leave a brace for her."

"Before you leave," Summer said quickly as he reached for his bag "could you look at Tarzan?"

"Sure. Who is Tarzan?"

"This is Tarzan," Biji said, indicating the fawn in her lap. "Dawn attacked him. His leg is hurt."

The doctor sat beside her. Summer climbed onto the bed anxiously. Biji released the deer for the doctor to see the leg that wasn't bent. Summer's heart thudded as she took in the little creature she'd spent weeks caring for. She'd wanted to beat Dawn senseless for harming such a vulnerable life.

The doctor took the leg gently and tested it. Tarzan squirmed and tried to escape.

"This looks like it's broken," the doctor said.

Summer's heart plummeted. "Can you fix him?"

"Well ..." He glanced at Amber. "I can put his leg in a brace. Baby aspirin will keep the pain and swelling down, but I'd recommend you get him to a vet this week. He'll need X-rays and probably a cast."

"Anything you can do, we'd appreciate," Amber said.

"Let me run to my car." He left the room.

Summer stroked Tarzan, pitying him. The little orphan had more issues than she did.

"You feeling okay?" Amber asked her.

"I'm fine. Just worried about Tarzan," Summer replied. "I'm so sorry about all of this."

"It's not your fault. There's likely to be some fallout, but dealing with issues seems to be my job description this week so far."

Summer glanced up at Amber's frustrated tone.

"I'll let you know tomorrow what will happen," Amber added.

"What do you mean?" Summer asked.

"Fighting is forbidden on the school grounds, even if for a good cause."

Summer felt cold inside.

"But you worry about Tarzan, and I'll worry about this," Amber said, smiling. "I will say this: you and Dawn won't be attending classes tomorrow. So stay here and take care of Tarzan, okay?"

Summer said nothing. She couldn't help feeling there was more of an issue than Amber let on. The Light arts instructor's gaze was troubled. Turning her attention to Tarzan, Summer calmed him from the doctor's manipulations of his leg. Biji was unusually quiet, as if she, too, sensed what Summer did.

The doctor returned with two braces, one for her and a child-sized air cast for Tarzan. He unwrapped the first brace and slid it on Summer's arm, over her swollen elbow. He then straightened the deer's leg and put the cast in place.

"Don't let him take this off," he warned. "Wear yours for an hour. Take it off, ice your elbow for twenty minutes, and then put it back on." He held up a small prescription bottle and a slender tube of balm. "Take one of these daily for the next week, probably before bed. They'll make you sleepy. Use the balm as needed."

"Thank you," Summer replied, accepting them.

"Thanks, Doc Aarons," Amber said. "Hopefully, we don't have to call you again tomorrow."

"Anytime, Amber." The doctor gathered his things and smiled at Summer and Biji before leaving. Amber closed the door behind her.

Summer followed, locking it. After Dawn's unexpected outburst, she wasn't taking any chances that someone else would come in uninvited.

"I hope he's okay," Biji said, caressing Tarzan's neck.

"Me, too. I'm really scared," Summer whispered. She sat beside her fawn. "I hope she doesn't send me back to LA."

"I don't think so. I mean, Dawn attacked you. How could she?"

"I don't know. I've learned that people don't usually care who started fights, though. I saw so many orphan kids thrown out of school for fighting bullies."

"Your birthday's in two days. Things like that don't happen on your birthday."

Summer smiled. "I hope you're right."

"I am. You belong here. They can't turn away a witchling, even if you were in a fight. Last year, Beck and Decker got in a huge fight. They almost killed each other, and they only got suspended for a week."

"I guess they could make me stay in my room for a week," Summer said, considering. "That wouldn't be too bad."

"You could take care of Tarzan."

"Yeah, I could," she said. She sighed. A week trapped in her room would suck, but not as bad as being thrown out of the school and sent back into the orphanage. Maybe Biji was right, and that was as far as the school would go. "It might actually be a good thing, because he'll need a lot of help for a while."

212

"See? It'll work out," Biji said, smiling. "I hope they expel Dawn, though."

"Me, too. You were totally right about her, Biji," Summer said bitterly. "She set me up at the dance. I bet she was the one who tried to poison Tarzan."

"When you go see Amber tomorrow, you have to tell her about those things," Biji advised. "It makes what she did seem less like she was acting out of passion and more like she planned it. I saw something like that on one of those crime shows on the telly, and the bad guy went to jail, because he had a history of harassing someone."

"I'm tired of being nice about it. No more," Summer said, thoughts going to what Decker told her about the curses. "I'll tell Amber everything tomorrow."

"Good. I hope it's enough for them to throw her out of school."

Determined, Summer rebuilt the pillow fort around Tarzan. Her thoughts went to Decker, and she wondered what issue had kept him from being with her. He and Amber both had looked at Beck strangely, and she guessed it had something to do with his black eye. Which meant it might have something to do with Dawn, too.

Remembering that Dawn had attacked two people in two days, Summer began to believe Biji was right. She was out of control, and the school would have to do something more than suspend her.

Her mind turned to Decker, and she grew anxious for him. She didn't know what transitioning into the Master of Fire and Night would encompass, but she doubted it'd be pleasant. She hoped she saw him before it happened and couldn't help the trickle of dread at the thought of seeing him   after.

Chapter Fifteen

SAM WOULDN'T BE found. Decker searched the creature's favorite haunts for two hours before giving up. The yeti didn't respond to his summons, even when he sent Beck back to the van to wait. Sam may have avoided him in the forest, but he wouldn't come sundown, when Decker's ceremony started. He spent the rest of his day calming Beck down. The shuttle took them to the mall and picked them up in time to return them both for Decker's ceremony.

His nerves were shaking already, his head throbbing from the clamoring spirits of the gathering Dark witchlings. The field where the Dark ceremony was held was nearly full. Dark witchlings had traveled from all over the world to witness his coronation.

"I don't see Mother, either," Beck said, scanning the field. "Something's going on."

Decker rubbed his temples.

The sun was gone from the sky, hidden behind the forest. Soon, the horizon would turn colors, indicating it was time to start the ceremony. The ceremony would last until just after midnight, the official start to his new duties. He looked towards the school again, wishing he'd seen Summer. His hand went to the birthday present he'd gotten for her in his pocket.

"I can't believe the school would do this to me," Beck said for the millionth time. "How can they stand in the way of my destiny?"

"I don't know, Beck," Decker replied. "The only thing I can figure out is Sam either told them to or they're waiting to talk to him about it. No one else could make them stop it."

"And Mother is just not even—"

"I know, I know."

Beck looked at him. "You look awful."

"I feel awful."

"I'll stay with you, Decker. I won't leave you like Aunt Nora did our mother."

"I know, Beck, thanks." Decker managed a smile. "We'll get your stuff straightened out, too."

"I wonder if we'll finally meet Nora at my ceremony."

"We'd be the first people in our family to see her in the past twenty years."

"She must really hate Mother," Beck mused. "I guess that's why she avoids us, too."

"Sometimes I understand why."

"Yeah, I do, too."

Matilda was in the center of the pentagram on a natural rise in the field. She waved to him. Decker straightened, glancing towards the sky. The signs of sunset had begun to spread. The field fell silent, except for the clamoring of his mind. Scared, he turned to Beck.

"If something happens and I explode or something …"

"You love me, want me to drive your Harley and take care of Summer." Beck rolled his eyes to ease the tension. "Okay."

"More or less," Decker said with a faint smile.

"Go get 'em."

Beck's confidence soothed him. Decker drew a deep breath and strode to Matilda. She stepped out of the pentagram as he stepped in. At once, the world around him silenced and the air vibrated. The spirits of those in the field were focused on him rather than on their own turmoil and created a hum that moved through him as easily as his magick.

He relaxed some, hoping this was what it felt like to become the Master. Maybe he wouldn't hear the sounds of souls the rest of his life, but would feel this calm at his center.

Just when he'd given up hope that Sam would appear, the auburn yeti melted out of the forest beside Beck. Decker saw his twin jump and turn to Sam, who rested a hand on his shoulder. Decker glanced around, gaze settling on the five points of the pentagram. Four of the five points had waist-high tiki torches holding black glass candle holders. In one was Earth. In another burned Fire. The third was empty to contain Air and the fourth was filled with Water.

The fifth point directly ahead of him was empty. Matilda began a cleansing ceremony, and the scents of herbs grew strong as she circled the pentagram. Those in the field were silent, watching. He felt his mother arrive before he saw her. He looked around, startled when she materialized ahead of him, at the fifth arm of the pentagram in the place where the fifth element—Spirit—belonged.

"Mother," he whispered, glancing towards Beck.

"We'll talk after." Her voice was firm. Her eyes were already filed with blackness.

Decker bit his tongue. He didn't quite know what to expect from her when she looked like this. The last time, she'd killed someone.

Matilda finished her circle and stepped back. His mother's magick unleashed around him, a black fog that blocked everything but the two of them. The hum of souls grew louder, stronger, and made his insides shake. She left her place at the head of the pentagram and stood before him.

"Most of this is for show. Sam would say humans are creatures that like tradition." she told him. "The true transition is simple." She held out her hand.

Decker's whole body shook from the vibrations. He took her hand. His ears buzzed and his body went limp. He passed out.

At least, he thought he did. He shook his head to clear it, not expecting to find himself on a cliff overlooking a wide, slow, winding river under a full moon.

"This is Nataniel, the Darkbringer, the first of our bloodline cursed with our magick." His mother stood beside him.

Disoriented, Decker looked around. The place felt real, from the cool ocean breeze to the sweet smelling grass. At the same time, he had the sense of being removed from the spot, as if he was watching it happen through a window. His attention went to the yeti standing in front of two men in cloaks with bows and spears standing twenty feet away. The

217

men looked like the Native Americans in picture books. They were talking, but Decker couldn't hear them.

The yeti held out his hand to one of them as Decker's mother had to him. The man took it and collapsed to his knees. Blue flames surged from the yeti into the man, who looked as if he was trying hard not to vomit. Black fog built around the man while the yeti spoke.

"He says, the only way to prevent evil is to become a part of it and use its own power to restrict it," his mother said quietly. "Nataniel lived another four years. His soul is the strongest of those you will inherit. His magick was pure. You will find it gives you strength when your own is lacking."

The black fog inched towards them and surrounded them. Decker heard the buzzing again and tried hard not to pass out. Images played through his mind of a life that wasn't his. Voices whispered Nataniel's secrets while Decker watched the vision of how Nataniel spent his four years as enforcer.

The fog cleared to show a similar scene next to a lake. This time, it was only the yeti and Nataniel's successor.

"Nataniel's son, Horus, was known to his own kind as the Peacebringer. His magick was like a candle in the night. He cast light upon anyone he came across, even those who could not be salvaged. He reigned for forty years," his mother said.

Blue flames coursed through Horus, and black fog burst from him as well. Decker closed his eyes, bracing himself for more images and voices whispering things he couldn't catch. By the time the fog cleared to show the third Master of Fire and Night, Decker was vomiting.

"It's a lot to take in," his mother said, kneeling beside him. "Don't try to remember anything. It'll be in your mind for you to recall and explore later. Every secret, every fear, every triumph of our predecessors will be yours to carry. The history of the Masters is vital, and their souls will give you strength."

"So I'll have the souls of all of them?" he asked, wiping his mouth.

"Yes. This is where our magick comes from."

"Why do I need to know their thoughts?"

"Their thoughts will keep you on the right path. It's easy to get lost in the Dark. They will anchor you, like a cheering squad."

"Zombie cheerleaders."

His mother chuckled. "Something like that. You'll find—when you feel completely alone and like you can't go another day—they'll help you."

"Did you ever feel that way?" Decker looked at his mother.

"Several times. I wanted to die. I never wanted to kill anyone. I never wanted to make anyone suffer. Everyone in my family thought Nora would go to the Dark and I would go to the Light. I was like Beck: carefree, harmless, and happy."

"What happened?"

"You'll see, son."

Decker saw the raw pain cross her face. He'd resented and feared her since she took his soul. He'd never considered what she might've gone through on her own in her role as the Mistress of Fire and Night. He'd never thought her capable of being vulnerable.

"We have a long way to go," his mother said. "Next up is Bartholomew the Terrible, the Deathbringer."

"Oh, god," he muttered. "The psycho."

"Maybe, maybe not."

Decker drew a deep breath and stood. His mother stood beside him. She'd made it through this; he could, too.

219

As they watched, Horus passed his magick onto the eighteen year old boy. Decker readied himself for the awful flood of scenes to follow, and as he expected, he was horrified to see what Bartholomew spent decades doing. The scenes ended with his violent death, where his sons found two amulets around his neck.

"One for him, one for the woman he couldn't kill," his mother said softly. "His only love. He chose a lifetime of madness over killing her."

"That's why he went mad?" Decker drew a sharp breath.

"Bartholomew was the first to reveal the weakness of our bloodline. While we were capable of handling more than any other human, we weren't invulnerable," she explained. "There were two things we had to balance: the evil around us and the evil within us."

They were somewhere else now, where Bartholomew's son met with the yeti. Beside him was a young woman who glowed with Light magick.

"We needed a counterbalance to keep from being consumed," Decker's mother continued. "A husband or wife from the Light who could keep us from falling completely to the night. Bartholomew's son, Tranin the Restorer, lived—"

"Wait," Decker said. "You're saying I *need* my uh … counterbalance? You and Father weren't just an anomaly?"

"No. We were meant to be together," she said with a smile.

"And nothing bad happens to whoever it is?"

"Nothing. The burden of dealing with the Dark is yours alone, but you'll have someone who quells your mind when she's near and makes life bearable."

For the first time since meeting Summer, hope flickered to life within him. They weren't doomed. He wouldn't put her in danger. They were meant to be together. Even better— they were expected to be together.

"There is someone," his mother said, studying him. "The girl from this weekend?"

"Yeah," he said softly, a smile crossing his features.

"Good. You won't end up like Bartholomew. That's been the big concern with you."

"It shouldn't be," he said. "Not anymore."

She smiled. "Then let's get through this. I want to meet this girl."

Decker was alive for the first time in months. He nodded and braced himself.

They went through the history of Dark Masters. He managed not to get sick again, though the images in his head and the scenes they visited made him nauseous more than once. The idea he didn't have to be alone, that he could have Summer, fed him strength to keep on his feet as his mother taught him about their history.

They reached the scene where her father, Louis, turned over the reins to her. Decker expected her transition to be the easiest of them all, for they'd live very quiet lives. Until he saw the images of what happened three days after she became the Dark Mistress.

He gasped, his eyes going to her. His mother's features were tight, pained, and she gazed into the fog instead of at him.

"That's why we never met Nora," he said at last, stunned.

"She was the Mistress of Light for three days," his mother replied in a hushed tone. "The reason she didn't become the Mistress of Night was because she was too weak. She couldn't withstand what this position required. I didn't think I was suited for this position, but the Dark claimed

221

me. She couldn't withstand what her own position required. I took her soul and killed her."

The calm words left him speechless. The black fog cleared from around them, revealing the vacant field again. It was morning. They sat in the center of the pentagram. The scent of herbs still hung in the air, and he sensed rather than saw Sam there somewhere. Beck was hunched against a tree, asleep.

"I thought there couldn't be a Dark without Light," Decker said at last. He didn't know what else to say, not when his mother just admitted to killing her twin. He thought of killing Beck and knew he couldn't do it.

"I took on both roles, protector and enforcer," she answered. "This is the reason the balance has swung to the Dark. The Mistress of Light has not existed in twenty years. There's been no one to grow the Light, but I've been killing, adding to the Dark."

Decker rubbed the back of his head. His mother appeared unruffled by her actions, and he couldn't help wondering if any part of her regretted her actions. Worse, would he become like her in twenty years? Immune to killing? Capable of killing those he loved most?

Would he care what he did if he could come home to Summer every night?

"And that is the final secret," she added. "You know all of them now, from the first Dark Master to the latest Dark Mistress."

His head swam with disjointed images and whispers from across time and different people's memories. She was right; he could make little sense of them. But they were there, and soon, they'd become a part of him as they had her.

"You will be able to explore your newfound powers. I can help you," she continued. "You'll know when it's time to claim a soul. I'll go with you the first time. I'll retain some of my powers. My father can still sense when a soul goes bad, so I think I can, too."

"Thanks, I think," he said. "I don't feel different."

"You will when you step outside the circle."

He gave the circle a leery look. He wasn't ready yet to leave the calm of the pentagram.

"About Beck," he said.

"I got your messages," she said. "And the school's. Your father spoke to the attorneys. He'll handle it. We intend to have the ceremony this week, with or without the school's permission. If it means your father shuts down the school and kicks everyone out, so be it."

Though he had a pliant temper and quick smile, Michael Turner never failed to get what he wanted. Decker relaxed at the thought his father had already made a decision regarding Beck's ceremony. The rest—mainly Dawn—seemed inconsequential after all he'd learned during his own ceremony.

At his silence, his mother rose. Decker remained, not feeling ready to face himself after all he'd learned. Of all he saw, he struggled most with his mother's actions.

"I'll give you some time," she said. "And have a talk with Beck."

"Thanks."

Decker watched her leave the safe place and cross to his twin. She shook him awake, and Beck woke with a grimace.

Decker's attention went back to his thoughts. He rested on his back and gazed at the midmorning sky. It was bright and clear. He should've felt torn, as he did before the ceremony. He feared his new duties, but he'd face them with Summer at his side. Remembering the peace that filled him when they were together, he closed his eyes and tried to make some sense of the knowledge and memories spinning in his head.

Over and over, he came back to his mother killing her twin. Disturbed, he stayed in the pentagram until the sun was almost directly overhead before he stood and reluctantly stepped outside.

The onslaught was worse than he expected. The magick she passed to him was overwhelming and drove him to his knees. Even with no one around, he heard souls.

"Easy," his mother said, taking his arm. She helped him up. "You'll need to rest for a few days."

"I want to see Summer," he managed. The world around him wobbled, a mix of colors and blurry shapes.

"Summer's her name? Fitting for the partner of a Dark Master. We can drop by the school on the way to the cabin. I doubt you'll be able to stay long."

"You made it!" Beck's voice held relief. He took Decker's other arm. "Thank God we're leaving. I could eat a yeti."

Decker smiled. He tried to force his feet to walk. He made it a few steps. He felt like he was flying and falling at the same time, like the pressure of magick within him would make him explode while the magick of the world would make him implode. The sensations were completely unbalanced, beyond his control.

By the time they made it to the car, he was able to walk slowly. As long as he didn't look around or lose his focus on his next step, he'd make it. He all but collapsed into the backseat of his mother's SUV and sucked in shaky breaths.

Beck got into the passenger seat and dug through a small cooler in the front seat.

"Here, Decker," he said and passed back a sandwich.

Decker ate it in three bites, unaware of how hungry he was until he smelled food. He and Beck wolfed down the lunch Louis packed them. By the time they'd finished, they reached the school.

"Beck has a restraining order," their mother said, eyeing her son. "He's not allowed in. You need your rest, Decker. Be quick, okay? We'll have your Summer over for dinner tomorrow."

"It's her birthday tomorrow!" Beck said cheerfully.

Decker was halfway out the door. He wobbled with his first step and spread his arms for balance. Excitement filled him, spinning quickly out of control like the rest of his magick. He reached the porch and reached for the railing to balance himself. Not wanting to fall over as soon as he saw Summer, he took a deep breath and struggled to balance the sensations pelting him from within and without.

At long last, he made it up the stairs and stood before her door. The effort left him near panting, and he steadied his breathing. Before he could raise his hand to knock, the door was wrenched open. Tiny Biji stood in the middle of the doorway, a raised bat in her hands. As soon as she saw him, she lowered it and stepped back.

Decker had no idea what he looked like after the rough night but suspected it wasn't good.

"Umm, it's for you, Summer. I'm gonna just step out," Biji said. She inched around him, taking the bat with her. Her gaze remained cautious.

Decker pushed the door open. Summer stared at him from across the room. Surprise then uncertainty crossed her

225

features. He closed the door, wishing he had a mirror to see what they saw. Finally, she rushed to him and flung her arms around him.

Decker stabilized. The sensations stopped and he thought of nothing but staying with her. He was warm.

"You made it!" she said at last, looking up at him.

"Barely," he said. He touched her swollen bottom lip gently with his thumb, agitated to see she'd been hurt by Dawn. Her cheekbone was bruised as well. Decker kissed her gently. "I can't stay long. My mother is waiting. I need to spend some time with her and Beck. But I wanted to give you your birthday present early and invite you to dinner tomorrow to meet my folks."

Summer glowed at his words and her singing soul was contagious. She raised herself to her tiptoes and fluttered kisses over his face. Heat rose within him, energizing him.

"We're going to be okay," he said as she kissed him. "I found out why we feel like we're meant to be together."

"Why?" she asked.

"Well, because we are. Every Dark Master has a perfect match, and you're mine."

"So we can be together."

"Yep."

Summer grinned and hugged him again. He breathed in her scent, thrilled to have her in his arms. He didn't want to leave her, but he had some learning to do. Knowing he didn't have to give up Summer made him regard his life differently. He didn't have to choose between his future and his heart. He didn't have to spend his life alone.

He pulled away and reached into his pocket for her birthday present.

"I got us both something. I figured when you turn eighteen we can get the real thing," he said and withdrew a small jeweler's pouch. He handed it to her.

Summer took it with a curious smile and dumped the two rings onto her palm. She gasped.

"Promise rings," he said. "One for you and one for me. It's not much, but I thought—"

"It's *perfect*!" she exclaimed. Her eyes gleamed with tears, and Decker smiled, his own throat tight.

"We said the words the other night," he said, taking the white band with a pink sapphire. "I meant it. I'm yours, Summer." He slid the ring over her ring finger.

"I'm yours, Decker," she whispered, sliding the white band with a black stone over his finger. "Forever."

"Forever."

She kissed him with heat that made his resolve slip. Decker pressed her against the wall, kissing her hungrily. His phone rang. With a groan, he pulled it out and saw it was his mother. He sighed and rested his forehead against Summer's. They were both breathing hard already.

"Tomorrow night," he promised. "You'll stay with me after dinner, okay?"

"Deal," she said. "Thank you, Decker." Her heart was in her words.

"You saved me, Summer," he replied. "But I know now everything will be okay."

"Thank god. I was afraid I'd lose you."

"Never." He kissed her and eased away. "I'll see you in the morning."

Chapter Sixteen

SUMMER WANTED TO scream out of happiness. She waited for the door to close then danced around her room, stopping finally to look at her ring. The tiny pink gem sparkled.

Though he was changed by the ceremony, Decker still wanted to be with her. He was more resolved than ever that they'd be together. She wasn't sure what erased his doubt and fear, but he'd been confident, hopeful.

She threw herself on the bed opposite Tarzan, beyond thrilled. Even if she did get suspended for a week, she had Decker. When she turned eighteen, they'd get married. He'd all but said the words. In a matter of a month, she'd found her home and her future.

Convinced her life had changed for the better, she admired her ring until Biji knocked on the door. Summer opened it and smiled at her little bodyguard.

"He looked different," Biji said instantly. "Way different."

"He did," Summer agreed. Decker appeared as he had at night, with shadows and darkness trailing him. For a moment, he'd seemed to flicker, as if he wasn't really there. "He did it, Biji. He's the Dark Master, and he says we can still be together."

"Wow," Biji murmured. She walked into the room and closed then locked the door behind her. "I heard something in the hallway."

"What?" Summer asked, seating herself near Tarzan again.

"Beck knocked up Dawn."

"No!"

"I overheard it," Biji said. "Something about her family suing his over it."

"That's weird." Summer frowned. Beck had pried her and Dawn apart yesterday, even taking some blows from the furious blond. He hadn't tried to protect Dawn. She wondered if Biji had misheard. "How or why would they sue over it?"

Biji shrugged. "Advance child support? I don't know. Is that a ring?"

Summer held up her hand. Biji took it and stared.

"It's a promise ring," Summer said. "One day, we'll get married."

"Summer, that's awesome! I'll come to your wedding. Tarzan can be the ring boy."

Summer laughed, eyes on the fawn. She petted him, hoping he'd be completely well one day.

"All we need is for Tarzan to get well, and I'll be happier than I've ever been before," she murmured.

229

There was a knock at her door. Biji picked up her bat and answered it, stepping aside to show Amber. The normally chipper instructor looked unhappy.

"Summer, could you come down to the office after dinner?"

"Sure."

"Great. How's he holding up?" Amber asked, eyes on Tarzan.

"Better today," Summer answered.

"I'm happy to hear that. All right, I'll see you around seven."

Amber left, and Summer exchanged a look with Biji.

"She didn't look happy," Biji said.

"No, she didn't."

"I wonder if she'll suspend you for like, two weeks."

"I don't know. Something has seemed off with her for a couple of days," Summer said, puzzled. "I wonder if the Dawn thing has her down."

"Beck was one of her favorite students."

Summer looked at her ring. Whatever happened, it wouldn't last long. Amber might suspend her for a week or two, but she could spend time with Tarzan and Decker.

Still, something about the look on Amber's face made her uneasy. Summer and Biji ate in shifts, so one of them could stay with Tarzan, Biji going down at six and Summer at half past six. Dawn, Decker and Beck weren't at dinner, and Summer made her way after dessert to Amber's office. She knocked and waited.

The taller, severe-looking Matilda opened the door.

"Come in."

Summer did. Amber sat in one of the armchairs and motioned Summer to the couch with a distracted smile. Her office was comfortable and cluttered, with no desk and an abundance of chairs and filled bookshelves.

"First, congrats on passing your test," Amber said. "Your trial was your Tarzan. You passed easily, as I knew you would."

Summer smiled in response.

"We have to postpone your ceremony, though, for the time being. We wanted to wait until Beck took his place as the Master of Light."

"I thought he did yesterday," Summer said.

"No. Decker went through his ceremony, but there have been some issues we're addressing," Matilda said carefully. "But rest assured, we'll bring you back for a ceremony, even if it's a few weeks down the road. We owe that to all witchlings who pass their trials."

"Bring me back?"

"That's the bad news. After the fight, Dawn's family filed for restraining orders against you and Beck. Neither of you are supposed to come within one hundred yards of her or the school," Amber said, her smile fading. "The school rules for fights are mandatory suspension of a week. We can suspend you in place, but not with the restraining order."

"I don't understand," Summer replied. "I didn't do anything to her. She attacked me."

"I know, Summer," Amber said.

"You're poor. That's the gist of this. Dawn's family has money and lawyers. Beck's does, too. His family is already countersuing for … for another issue, however, there's no one to defend you," Matilda said. Frustration made her pace. "You're one of our best students, and Sam adores you. When this blows over, you can come back."

"Come back from where?" Summer demanded, starting to panic. "You're sending me back to the orphanage?"

Amber said nothing, and Matilda looked away.

231

"When?"

"Tomorrow morning," Matilda said after a long pause. "Bus leaves at seven."

"On my birthday. You're throwing me out on my birthday."

"We will bring you back," Amber said firmly. "It might take awhile, but we will."

It might take awhile. They were throwing her out, like every other school she'd been to. Summer's face grew hot. She'd thought this place was different.

"Please don't worry," Amber went on. "It might take a month or two. As soon as we've got some way of righting this, we'll drive to LA and bring you back. I promise."

Decker. Her breath caught. She rose. Without a word to them, Summer ran out of the office and back to her room. She slammed the door and paced, oblivious to Biji and Tarzan.

She couldn't leave without Decker. She'd only just found him and grown happy here.

"What's wrong?" Biji asked.

"They're sending me back to the orphanage." Her words were quiet. She wanted to scream but found herself slipping into a familiar zone where she felt nothing.

It was just one more school. One more failure. Summer squeezed her eyes closed.

"What? No! How can they do that?" Biji demanded, distraught.

"Dawn … filed a restraining order. I can't come to school, because she's here. I guess there's nowhere else to send me but back to LA."

"I hate that bitch! But what about Decker?"

"I don't know." Summer rose again. "He's supposed to come in the morning, but I have to leave in the morning, too."

"What time are you supposed to leave?"

"Seven."

"You and Decker went to breakfast at six thirty, right?" Biji's brow crinkled as she thought hard.

"Yeah."

"Then when he comes, you can tell him. He'll take you to his house."

"Biji, they've told the orphanage," Summer whispered. "Amber said they'd send me back until things cooled off then bring me back here. If I don't go, the orphanage won't let me come back."

"It's not fair! How can that bitch run you off?"

Because I'm nobody. Summer wept inside. Matilda was right; Summer had no family or money to defend herself. She had nothing, not even a compelling reason for them to bring her back. She'd passed their trial and was now a member of the Light. They didn't need her here. An hour ago, she'd had a home, a boyfriend, a future.

Now, there was nothing again. She never remembered feeling devastated at the reality of her situation before. This time, she did.

"I'll just tell him farewell in the morning," she said. "He'll have two more years here, and I'll be out of the orphanage when I'm eighteen in a year. If he doesn't hate me for leaving, maybe then ..."

A year was a long time.

"That's ridiculous. He gave you a promise ring, Summer. It means he loves you."

233

"I love him, too. But I've got nothing, Biji. No family, no money, no future. Maybe it's better this way."

"What is wrong with you?" Biji asked, shaking her. "It is not better this way! Decker loves you and you love him. All you have to do is tell him. Right now. Take the shuttle and go see him. I'll stay with Tarzan."

"The shuttle," Summer breathed. "I can go to him tonight!"

"Right now."

"Oh, god, Biji, you're brilliant!" Summer sprang up. While she doubted Decker could do anything for her, she could at least find comfort in his arms and reassurance that he'd be there for her in a year, when she was free of the orphanage.

Hands shaking, Summer pulled on a sweatshirt and flew down the stairs. The shuttle was just starting to pull away when she threw open the front door. She waved it down, and it stopped.

"Store?" the driver asked.

"No, the beach," Summer replied.

"A little late for a swim, isn't it?"

"I won't be there long."

"How about you, miss?"

Summer turned to see the Dark girl in the back of the van. She recognized the slender teen with bright blue eyes from dinner but didn't know her name.

"Resort for a hotdog," the girl replied.

"They have great hotdogs."

Summer fidgeted all the way to the beach. She hopped out of the van. Too worried to notice the other girl didn't leave the van, Summer took off at a jog down the dirt road leading around the south side of the lake. Dark fell completely over the forest. Breathless, her pace slowed. The trees leaned down to touch her, and she reached up when she thought of it to touch the pines. She no longer felt threatened in the forest, not when the trees and wind were eager to talk to her.

Her magick grew within her, even if it couldn't connect yet with the outside world. The tinkle of air and low thrum of the earth were louder this evening, as if they crept closer to her to talk to her. They made her feel less like her world was crashing down on her.

Struck by the thought, Summer stopped and gazed around her. If she went back to LA, she'd lose the connection to nature. There'd be no trees to high-five her, no free breezes to mess up her hair. She'd lose so much more than the school. She'd lose herself again.

Tears bubbled. Summer looked around and wiped them away. For a moment, she thought she'd seen someone following her. When she could see clearly, nothing was there. Summer hurried down the path and branched off onto the winding road leading to Decker's home. The garage door was closed and the house ablaze with light.

She went to the back door and rang the doorbell. The idea of seeing Decker made her antsy, and she paced until the door cracked open. An African-American man with white hair opened the door. While small, his expression was severe.

"May I help you?" he asked.

"I'm looking for Decker," she replied.

"You came all the way from the school after dark?"

"Yes. It's kinda important I see him."

"Young Decker is out with his girlfriend. But if you'd like to come in, I can call him to come home."

"Oh, no. I mean, his girlfriend?" she asked blankly.

"He left a few hours ago with her. Alexis, Alex, something like that."

Alexa. Summer's blood ran cold. She twisted the ring on her finger. Decker had been dating someone else before, but she didn't think he could lie about his feelings for her.

"Shall I call him?" the small man prompted.

"No. Thanks. I'll catch him at school." Summer turned away, not at all certain what to think about the strange words.

Maybe that's why he didn't bring me home with him tonight, she couldn't help thinking. But it wasn't possible he'd cheat on her. Or maybe *everything* here was an illusion. Amber's assurances she'd fit in and be able to stay, Dawn's curses and tricks, maybe even Decker ...

No. Everything else might have been an illusion, but what she and Decker felt for each other was solid. They'd spent their first two nights together here, in his room.

At least I have Biji and Tarzan. Lost in her thoughts, she made her way back to the beach to wait for the shuttle. The lake was silent, the only light coming from the resort. Summer gazed at the deck where she and Decker had realized what each meant to the other. This place was as screwed up as any of the others she'd been to. But Decker was the one constant. No matter what the man at his house said.

Summer sat near the sidewalk, troubled. She was empty, and the cheerful wind did nothing to soothe her. The ground beneath her grew warm again when she shivered. Her thoughts were dark, her gaze going to the ring on her hand.

Decker loves me, she told herself over and over. *Will he love me enough to wait a year?*

She didn't know the answer. She wasn't even certain she would find him before she left.

236

Summer wrapped her arms around her knees. The shuttle came around ten, and she climbed into the passenger seat. The world whipped by. She wasn't sure she'd ever see this place again. Its magick would be gone, and she'd be alone in the world, as usual.

This place had been a temporary vacation, nothing more. There was no place for her in this world.

Despondent, Summer trudged to her room. Biji and Tarzan were both gone, and she assumed her only friend had taken the fawn to her room to sleep. Summer lay on her bed for a long moment. No part of her was tired. No part of her wanted to sleep the last few hours she had in the only place she'd almost felt was home.

She rolled onto her bed. It was an hour until her birthday, and she'd be cast away from the only peace she knew.

"Some birthday present," she muttered, eyes watering again.

"Summer?" Biji called then knocked.

Summer forced herself up and answered the door. Biji stood outside.

"Hey, how'd it go?" her friend asked.

"He wasn't there," Summer said, not wanting to relive her doubt and pain. She moved away from the door and threw herself onto the bed.

"Really? I thought that's where he went," Biji said, closing the door.

"The guy who answered the door said he was out with Alexa."

"No!"

Summer sighed.

"You don't think ... you think he's cheating?" Biji asked.

"I don't think so, Biji. But it's strange, isn't it?"

Biji was quiet, pensive. Summer gazed at her, hoping the resourceful girl had some sort of information on what might be going on.

"He gives you a promise ring then goes to meet with her after you get kicked out of school." Biji shook her head. "This has got to be the worst birthday ever."

"You don't think he would, do you?" Summer asked.

"I want to think no. But he was sleeping with her like, even up to the day before the dance. Ana said she saw them going off into the woods together. And suddenly, she's back in the picture? It doesn't seem like a good thing."

"No, it doesn't." Summer didn't know what to think. "I guess it doesn't matter. I leave in the morning. I'll probably never see any of you again."

"How can you say that? You're my friend!"

"Biji, I have nothing. I'm being sent away tomorrow. What do you think happens? The orphanage has never sent me to the same school twice, and in a year, I'll be kicked on my own. I have no family, no money, nothing!"

"I'll go with you."

"No, Biji, you can't come with me. People ... people love you." Summer began to cry, unable to help her heartbreak. Biji sat down and hugged her hard.

"I will kill him," Biji whispered fiercely. "I don't care if he is the Master of Night. I will find him and I'll kill him!"

"Just take care of Tarzan," Summer said, trying hard to stifle her tears. She'd never cried upon being cast out of any other school. She had to find a way to go numb again, to forget everything and everyone who touched her while she was here.

"I will. Where is he?" Biji looked around.

"I thought he was with you."

Biji frowned.

"Sometimes he goes in the closet," Summer said. She wiped her face and rose, crossing to the closet. Biji went with her.

When she opened it, a note fluttered to the ground. Biji retrieved it, reading aloud,

"You took everything that mattered to me. I did the same for you."

Summer looked at the note then in the closet. "Tarzan isn't here. Where is he, Biji? I left him with you."

"I came back to check on you awhile ago. You were here, and I left Tarzan with you," Biji answered.

Not my sweet Tarzan! Summer quelled her panic.

"I got back like, ten minutes before you came here," she said. "Biji, I wasn't here. I didn't get Tarzan back from you!"

Biji stared at the clock. "It was ten. I swear, Summer, you were sitting on your bed. I brought him back and you asked me to come back in a little bit."

"It wasn't me, Biji!" Summer seized the note.

"You think Dawn ... you think she used magick to hide herself?"

"Oh, god, we have to find him! He's vulnerable. He can't even walk!" Summer pulled on her shoes and sweatshirt. She yanked the door open and ran down the stairs.

"Wait, I'm coming with you!" Biji cried.

Emotions and magick churned within her. Summer hopped off the porch and stood still, listening. She closed her eyes.

Please, please tell me where he is! she begged the wind.

The magick within her stirred but was wild as ever. The tinkling of the wind grew louder, however, and pushed her towards the road that hugged the school property before branching out to the creek.

Summer ran down the road. The wind nudged her towards the forest next, and she charged in. Fear and adrenaline made her immune to the branches tripping and smacking her. Her thoughts were on Tarzan, the only innocent creature in this horrible place. He alone hadn't betrayed her. He alone hadn't destroyed what hope she had of finding a home or happiness!

Biji shouted from somewhere behind her.

Summer ran, blinded by desperation and anger. Her magick rose up within her, crouched, and then dove, colliding with the magick of the forest. She fully connected with the earth and air for the first time. Her senses were alive, like when she touched Decker. Her feet bounced off the earth as if it were rubber, and the air in her lungs left her energized rather than tired.

She reached a clearing and stopped to look, her breathing loud in her ears. Something lay on a large, flat rock that seemed out of place in the middle of the field crowded with wildflowers. Dread sank into her stomach. She ran to the rock and dropped on it, horrified.

Tarzan lay wheezing on the rock. His blood looked like black oil in the dim light of a new moon and flowed over the rock to the ground below. There were puncture wounds all over his body while his injured leg still wore the cast.

"No, no, no, Tarzan!" she whispered, trying to figure out how to pick him up without hurting him.

Someone had done this on purpose. The wounds weren't consistent with those of the mountain lion that killed his mother. These looked as if he'd been stabbed. She touched him. Her magick felt his pain, and tears crowded her eyes again.

"You can't die, my sweet Tarzan! You're all I have left!"

Hastily wiping away tears, she pulled off her sweatshirt and placed it over him. Summer lifted him carefully. The deer cried out in pain. She tried to shush it, but before she reached the forest, Tarzan's cries were too much for her to bear. Summer sank to the ground, shaking. She put him down and lifted the sweatshirt, staring at the blood that marred his body.

You must let him go. Sam's voice came to her.

"He's all I have," she replied. "I can't."

It is the way of things. You can do nothing.

"You said I healed him with my magick. I can use my magick now; I can heal him again!"

He's too far gone.

"No!" She started to cry and stroked the deer. "He doesn't deserve this. I deserve to lose everything, but he doesn't!"

You've lost nothing this night. His soul will return to the forest. You will feel him as you do the rest of the creatures in the forest.

Sam's words comforted her. Summer kissed Tarzan's small face. His eyes had gone glassy, his cries hoarse. His breathing was slowing.

Her sweet Tarzan was dying. Was this her fate too? To die alone, the victim of a world that wouldn't accept her?

The earth beneath them was warm. Summer noticed it grow hotter as her anger rose.

Come. He is lost.

"No. I won't leave him." Instead, she fed more energy into the earth. She did as Decker had taught her and pulled the magick towards her, until the thrum of the earth became a low roar.

Summer, you must step away. Sam's voice grew urgent.

"I won't lose him. I won't let anyone destroy him the way they've destroyed me!" she replied and placed both hands on the ground.

Magick intoxicated her, swirling from her, through her, into her. The earth and air responded, both trembling around her.

Tarzan stopped breathing. His eyes closed and his chest stopped moving.

He's gone. You must leave him.

Summer closed her eyes. She focused on building the magick then on the fawn's lifeless body. The earth rumbled. The air grew to a wail, its glitter surrounding her and the deer. Her magick burned bright as daylight.

"Bring him back to me!" she ordered the elements.

Summer, no! You can't—

"Bring him back!"

Her magick faded from bright white to black shadows that licked at the deer's body.

"Summer!" Biji's cry was terrified.

Summer felt only magick. It replaced her fear and emotions, swelling within her. She pulled and channeled it into Tarzan, her insides screaming in pent-up pain. Now that Tarzan was dead, she had nothing more to live for.

"Bring him back to me!" she shouted into the roaring elements.

What sounded like a thunderclap sounded and suddenly, there was silence. Summer collapsed, breathing hard. She stared at Tarzan.

"What did you do?" Biji whispered, drawing near.

Tarzan's body thrashed suddenly. The fawn screamed in pain. Summer reached for him, uncertain what was wrong. It clambered to its feet and bucked, alternately galloping and falling as it raced around the field.

His scream pierced through her. She chased him, trying to figure out why.

You brought him back from the dead. Now his soul is trapped between the forest and the corporeal world.

At the words, Summer slowed.

His pain is unlike any pain you have ever suffered.

Summer stopped, feeling sick to her stomach. She'd never heard such a sound before.

"Tarzan! Come here, Tarzan!" she shouted to the deer.

It crashed into a tree, wobbled to its feet, and began running again. She watched him, horrified.

"What's wrong with him?" Biji asked, running to her. "He sounds like he's in awful pain."

The worst pain in existence, Sam told Summer. *You've torn his soul in two. You've condemned him forever.*

Summer dropped to her knees. "I just wanted my friend back!"

At what price? His suffering?

"No ... I ..." She planted her hands on the ground again. "I'll fix it. I'll free him."

The elements answered more readily this time. Summer closed her eyes as she freed her magick. Soon, they were at a roar.

"Take him," she whispered to the earth. "Put him at peace."

Another thunderclap, and the field was silent again. She didn't see Tarzan anywhere.

"What exactly did you do?" Biji's voice held a note of fear.

Summer hung her head, empty. She hadn't even been able to save her only friend.

"Summer?"

Biji walked into her view. Summer was numb and cold. Unable to shake the image of Tarzan bleeding to death or the sounds of his screams, Summer wobbled to her feet.

"I tried to save him," she said. "I failed."

"Your magick is black."

Summer looked down at herself. Shadows clung to her as they did Decker.

You broke the Light Laws. You broke the Dark Laws. Sam's voice was sad. *The Master of Fire and Night will have no choice in what he does to right this.*

She no longer cared.

Chapter Seventeen

DECKER FELT THE slap his mother said he'd feel when a soul went bad. He roused himself from his bed and sat, trying to identify the sensations in his head. Dressing, he pulled open the door just as his mother was getting ready to knock.

"This one is bad," she said. "You feel it?"

"I do. I still can't quite sort through all this stuff in my head," he said.

"Focus hard. You'll be able to identify which laws were broken."

He closed his eyes. The slap continued, the stinging sensations painting a blurry scene. He saw Light then Dark magick, heard screams.

"Necromancy," he said, surprised. "Death."

"Someone tried to raise something from the dead then realized it tears the soul in two," his mother said. "This happens almost every time someone uses magick with the dead, which is why it's forbidden even for Dark witchlings."

"So they panic and kill it using magick," he guessed.

"One Light Law, one Dark Law broken."

"The penalty is their soul then death." His mouth felt dry. "Lucky me. First time out, and I get a double whammy."

"Better than my first night out," she reminded him.

He couldn't forget what she'd done to her twin.

"Let's go," she said, stepping aside.

Decker swallowed hard.

"I'll take us, since you might put us on the moon." She offered her hand. "I'll teach you some things about teleportation tomorrow. You've got a lot to learn about your new powers."

"Assuming I survive this."

"You will. The first time is the hardest."

When it was over, he'd run straight into the arms of Summer. He'd intended to do that this evening, when an unexpected visit from Alexa interrupted the family dinner. Furious at her, he'd agreed to go for a ride to get her away from his family, where he could interrogate her at will about her involvement in trying to burn his house down.

He'd gotten nowhere, because he couldn't use the gift his mother had for determining truth yet. After an hour-long argument, he left Alexa at the school and came home.

"Let's do this," Decker said, drawing a deep breath. He took his mother's hand.

After the walk through family history, her ability to transport them elsewhere no longer caused him discomfort. When the black magick cleared, he stood in a field that looked too familiar. The slab in the center marked it as the one he used to rendezvous with Alexa.

Whoever had done these things, he probably knew them. He turned, catching site of Biji first. Sam lingered in the forest. Biji looked panicked, but she glowed with Light, not Dark magick.

"Biji?" he called. "What's wrong?"

Biji looked at him then past him. Decker turned and froze.

Summer stood a few short feet away, black fog billowing off her. Her face was marred by tears. He was first struck by the power that flowed off her. Sam said she'd be strong, and he was right.

It took a lot of magick to raise something from the dead.

Decker felt as if his body was stabbed with ice. Summer was as frozen as he was, as if waiting to see what he'd do. He couldn't believe she stood before him let alone imagine what happened in the hours they were apart that led them to this.

"Go ahead, son," his mother said quietly. "Claim the amulet first."

Decker stepped towards Summer. He wondered if this was a trial for him as the new Master, if Summer and his mother were working together to test him. Because Summer wasn't capable of evil.

"I need your ... your amulet," he whispered then added silently, *please, please let this be a cruel joke!*

Summer paled. A look of soul-deep loss crossed her features. He'd seen the same on the faces of those his mother had claimed, but the look on the face of his Summer made him sick. A look of pain that deep couldn't be faked. This wasn't a joke or a trial.

"It'll be okay," he said. His words sounded weak to his ears. Her sins were like jackhammers in his head, the voices of all who came before him demanding he take her amulet and kill her.

All the voices, except one. Decker touched his temple, the sensations overwhelming. Bartholomew the Terrible alone was quiet in his mind.

Woodenly, Summer removed her amulet and held it out to him. Decker took it. He searched the memories of his predecessors for some other alternative to claiming her soul. His body broke out in a sweat despite the chilly night as Summer's haunted eyes gazed up at him. He held up the whiskey-colored crystal holding the soul of the girl who was supposed to spend her life with him.

This couldn't be happening.

Summer started crying, and his resolution broke. His mother had killed her twin, but Decker couldn't— wouldn't—hurt the only creature on the planet who'd ever accepted him for what he was.

Summer whirled and ran. Decker watched her, startled. The trees and wind parted the forest for her then closed behind her, swallowing her.

"Son," his mother said, drawing near.

The jackhammer in Decker's mind grew stronger. He felt the hunger his mother described, the need to consume his prey. He lowered Summer's soul to his side and shoved it in his pocket. His mother said something else, but he could only think of Summer.

Decker ran after her. The forest didn't part for him as it had for her, and his magick was as scrambled as his emotions. He fought his way through the thicket, adrenaline driving him. He needed to find her, to grab her and silence the voices and magick in his body. They'd figure out something, some way to let her live. There had to be something, because he wasn't ready to live without her.

His own tears rose as he tore through the forest after her. Branches seemed almost to be blocking him. Finally, he assembled enough control over himself to shove his magick forward. The trees parted for him as they had for her, and he saw her dead ahead of him, standing with her back to him.

Panting, Decker broke free of the forest and stopped. Summer stood at the edge of Miner's Drop, where he'd taken her to watch the moon rise. Her shoulders shook with sobs, and a newfound panic filled Decker.

"Summer, don't! It'll be okay. I can make it okay!" he said, aware of the wild desperation in his voice.

"You can't fix this," Summer said and turned to face him. She drew shaky breaths and wiped her face. "This is easier for us both."

"I can. I will. I swear it, Summer. If I have to quit, I will. We'll go somewhere, just you and me, and be happy."

"You can't quit."

"I'll find a way."

"I've lost everything." The hollow look crossed her face. "Even you."

"No, Summer!" he said. His heart slammed into his chest, and hot tears rolled down his face. "You haven't lost me. I'm here. It's just you and me right now."

"I don't want to die but I can't live knowing … I can't!"

"Please, please, just come with me. Trust me. We'll fix this. We'll be together," he begged. "Please, Summer." He held her gaze, willing her to trust him one more time. Decker raised his hand to her as he had many times before.

"I love you, Decker," she whispered.

249

"I love you, too, Summer." He stepped forward cautiously, one foot at a time.

She took his hand, and he closed the distance between them, hugging her hard. Summer sobbed, and Decker's mind quieted. Her magick whipped through him. He had no idea what he'd do, but he couldn't live without Summer. He held her, his tears wetting her soft hair.

"Come on," he said. "We're going home. I know someone who might be able to help us." His senses tingled, indicating magick. When he started to move away from her, Decker tripped and was propelled forward, out of his control.

As if in a dream, he saw the look of horror cross Summer's face as he careened into her. They toppled over the cliff. The sensation of weightlessness was quickly countered by a yank so sharp, it stole his breath.

Summer was torn out of his grip. He heard her scream even as he was jerked back onto the top of the cliff to safety. He scrambled forward, fighting whatever magick held him in place.

"Summer!" he shouted. Frantic, Decker tried to dive off the ravine wall after her. He clawed at the earth to drag himself forward but the magick crushed him to the ground.

Her screams stopped suddenly. Decker squeezed his eyes closed, knowing she'd hit the rocky slopes of the ravine wall. He roared in pain and fury, his magick going wild within him as he strained to move. He fought until sorrow crashed over him and he lay spent, sobbing on the ground.

The magick released him then. Too weak to move, Decker lay still, panting. The jackhammer sensation was still in his mind, though the voices of his predecessors had fallen silent.

"That was Summer."

"Get away from me," he whispered to his mother. "This is all your fault! You made me into this monster."

For once, she was quiet. Decker shivered as the cold night air robbed his body of heat. He sensed the presence of Sam as well. He hoped they left him there to die in the night, alone. Closing his eyes, he lay listless, the image of Summer falling filling his mind.

The former Mistress of Fire and Night rose from her crouch near her son. He wasn't moving. His breathing was labored, his face wet with tears. Decker hadn't cried since he was ten, even when she took his soul.

But Decker wasn't what disturbed her.

Instead, she turned to the forest. Something had happened here that didn't make an ounce of sense, even if the results were that the broken soul was dead. She'd placed a spell on Decker to keep him from going over the cliff. By the looks of his crumpled form, he wasn't about to run off on her.

As if sensing her anger, Sam disappeared. Rania knew where to find the elusive yeti after years of seeking him out for advice and went after him, appearing in his favorite hiding place before he did. When Sam arrived, his shoulders sagged. He refused to look at her but sat in his corner of the cave. Soon after coming into her powers at the age of eighteen, she'd sought refuge from killing her sister with Sam. She addressed him in the yetis' soft, guttural tongue.

"What's going on, Sam?" she asked calmly.

"It's done. It doesn't matter now," he replied.

"So you throw my son off a cliff and expect me to accept your answer?"

Sam sighed deeply. "It wasn't supposed to happen this way."

Rania drew closer. She sat in front of him, waiting with a predator's patience. Sam shifted under her direct gaze.

"I wasn't going to let him fall," he said at last. "But the girl, she had to. He wasn't going to do it."

"You couldn't leave this to me?"

He shook his massive head. A haunted look crossed his face. Rania knew there was too much he was keeping from her. She kept her own anger in check.

"This Summer girl, she was his partner, wasn't she?" she asked. "Like Michael is mine."

"Yes."

"She went Dark and broke Dark Laws. Even if her sentence was death, Decker could've postponed it."

"That was my fear."

"You'd rather turn him into another Bartholomew?"

"No, Rania. I love you all as I love the children of my forest," Sam replied. "I wish none of you harm, but … Rania, there was a time before time when evil you cannot imagine ruled this earth."

"I know this. It's how my family was chosen to enforce the Laws."

"That evil and that time were nothing like the evil of long ago." Sam rose and paced. "The evil my people fought many tens of thousands of years ago wiped out a civilization much like yours. It took a thousand years of war to contain it. I can't let that happen again."

"What does that have to do with Summer?"

"Your bloodline is descendent from an older bloodline, one that used to enforce Dark magick before this evil destroyed everything. The evil was unleashed when all five elements were joined in the Dark."

Rania listened, puzzled.

"Your ancestor, a Dark Master, held the elements of Water, Fire, and Spirit. His partner held the Air and Earth," Sam explained. "She fell to the Dark soon after they were together. Rather than forsake her, he did as Decker did and swore to let her live. We don't know what happened exactly, except the evil between them grew until it consumed them and everything around them. Thus, the partners of the Dark Masters and Mistresses have always been Light, since Nataniel took over the duties."

"Summer was Air and Earth," Rania guessed. "And so you have condemned my son to madness, like Bartholomew. What if the line ends with him, Sam?"

"It has been my study of mankind that men always fall victim to the weakness of temptation. Like Bartholomew, Decker will father twins someday."

Rania rose, fury building within her. "You know there is a way out of the Dark."

"It's never been done."

"But it exists. It wouldn't exist if it weren't possible!"

"You're not being logical, Rania. It is safer to condemn Decker than the world."

"He's my son, Sam!"

"You killed your sister. You know the price one of your bloodline pays."

"I do," she said, meeting his gaze. "I also know we pay it unwillingly, even as it kills everything we are."

"A small sacrifice for the fate of the world."

She turned away, aware he'd never fully understand what a sacrifice it was to serve the Dark. When it was her heart,

253

her soul, dying, she could bear it. When it was the heart of her son ...

"She had to die, Rania," Sam repeated sadly. "I liked her very much, more so because what she did was to save one of my children."

"She broke the laws for a forest creature?"

"She did. There was no malice in her actions."

"Yet you believe she couldn't be salvaged. You wouldn't even offer her the chance to recover her soul."

"It's never been done. It doesn't matter now anyway."

"I ran across something else that should've been impossible," Rania countered. She withdrew a small envelope from her pocket and held it out to Sam. It contained the hair she'd kept from Istvan's amulet the night she took the twins with her on her rounds. "One of the Dark witchlings was able to evade me."

Sam pulled the hair free and held it up to the light. "This is your hair?"

"It is. It was wrapped around the amulet of someone who went Dark. I think it kept me from tracking him."

"Possible," Sam said, puzzled. "I can research this with the other Sams."

Rania's mind worked quickly. Sam hadn't denied the ability of someone to evade a Dark Mistress, just as he hadn't denied there was a chance for redemption for Dark witchling. A trickle of hope went through her. Maybe there was much more the yetis knew that they'd never shared, even with her. Maybe there was another way to help her son.

Not that it would make a difference tonight. No one survived a swan dive off the top of Miner's Drop. Decker would spend the rest of his life unbalanced, alone, hurting. Taking her sister's life destroyed her. Only Michael saved her from madness. Decker's path was tragic enough without anyone there to give him hope that tomorrow might be better. What emotions she retained after a lifetime of Dark and death churned at the thought of her son suffering a worse fate than hers. She had to find a way to help him.

Her phone rang, startling her out of her thoughts. Rania started to reject the call when she saw Amber's name cross the screen. She answered it.

"Mrs. Turner?" Amber's voice held a note of alarm. "I just got a call from Biji, one of the girls at the school. She says she found Decker unconscious near Miner's Drop. We've called the ambulance but—"

"I'm on my way," Rania said calmly and hung up. She glanced at Sam again.

The yeti seemed genuinely sad about what he'd done. Rania sat. She didn't know what to do. There was no way to right what happened. When she felt ready to face Decker and the chaos likely to greet her at the ravine, she drew a deep breath and rose. Sam said nothing as she walked out of his cave and into the night.

The sounds of an ambulance and sirens wailed. Rania walked back to the top of the cliff, not wanting to alarm anyone by using her magick. She took her time, struggling for some sort of action she could take, something she could do for Decker. No words would help him. No amount of time would heal this wound.

She reached her son before the paramedics tearing through the forest. The little girl who had been in the field was leading them. Rania knelt beside Decker and touched his face. His skin was clammy and hot, his body shaking as if from fever chills. He clutched something in his hand. It was on a thin silver chain.

Rania tugged it loose and sat back, not surprised to see her son hadn't been able to crush the amulet of the girl he loved. What surprised her was the faint glimmer in the center of the amber amulet. Barely discernible, it was there nonetheless.

Rising to her feet, Rania peered into Miner's Drop. Her mind began to work in a new direction, one that just might save her son. She lifted the amulet again to double check the faint flicker of light was still there. Where there was light, there was life.

Somehow, Summer had survived the fall.

If you enjoyed this book, please consider leaving a review! Word of mouth is crucial to an author's success, and I'll be grateful for your time and assistance. In fact, if "Dark Summer" reaches 100 reviews before the second book is due out, I'll release the second book early! In addition, I'll be placing all reviewers in a pool for drawings to win autographed paperbacks every two weeks! Check out my website starting September 1 for winners.

Drop by my website
(http://www.GuerrillaWordfare.com/)

or my Facebook page
(http://www.Facebook.com/LizzyFordBooks/)

and let me know what you think!

Witchling Trilogy
Dark Summer (August 2012)
Autumn Storm (late 2012)
Winter Kiss (2013)